"I told Dad I'd asked you to marry me."

"And what did he say?" Sarah felt as if her life hinged on Mark's words.

"He asked if you'd said yes."

She urged him to go on with her eyes.

"I said you had."

"Why?" Sarah asked, horrified.

"Because you did agree," Mark said, smiling, his blue eyes gleaming mischievously.

"You *shouldn't* have told him!"

Val Daniels says she'll try anything once, from waitress to market researcher, from library aide to census coordinator. But her real love has always been writing. It was fitting that her first published novel, *Silver Bells*, was a Christmas romance, because her grandmother always used to put a Harlequin Romance in Val's Christmas stocking! Val lives with her husband, two children and a "Murphy dog" in Kansas.

Books by Val Daniels

FOREVER ISN'T
LONG ENOUGH
Val Daniels

Harlequin Books

TORONTO • NEW YORK • LONDON
AMSTERDAM • PARIS • SYDNEY • HAMBURG
STOCKHOLM • ATHENS • TOKYO • MILAN
MADRID • WARSAW • BUDAPEST • AUCKLAND

ISBN 0-373-03377-X

FOREVER ISN'T LONG ENOUGH

First North American Publication 1995.

CHAPTER ONE

'GET your hands off me.' Sarah Fields' coat missed the rack she was trying to hang it on as she turned on her boss. The man had just draped his arm around her shoulder again and dangled his hand as low as he possibly could get it.

'A little touchy, aren't we?' Her boss's leering grin dimmed a fraction of a watt as he caught her expression.

'No, Len, I'm tired.' She pushed past him, facing away from him in case he tried his other trick—the one where he didn't allow quite enough room between them so that she had to brush against him as she went by.

'What's the matter?' His arm came over her shoulder again.

She shrugged it off and clenched her teeth. 'I'm serious as a heart attack. I'm tired of pretending that you aren't trying to sneak a feel every chance you get.'

Len held up both hands and backed off two steps. 'Whoa! Don't get so excited, honey. I'm an affectionate kind of guy. I treat all you girls like you were my sisters.' The sloppy jowls on his face tightened slightly.

'Then I hope you don't have a sister.' Sarah glared at the assistant manager of the Pancake Palace. 'And I'm not the only one who is sick of dodging your overactive hands.'

5

Len's eyes hardened. 'You sound like you're making an accusation.'

Sarah realized she was protesting a little less tactfully than she had intended. 'I . . . I would just appreciate your keeping your affectionate gestures to yourself.'

'Oh, you would, would you?' He was red-faced and angry over the confrontation, but obviously realized she was backing down. He puffed his sagging midsection a few inches above his belt. 'Just a reminder, Miss High-and-Mighty. *You* came here looking for this job. We didn't come lookin' for you.'

He hitched the waist of his pants up and sauntered toward the front of the restaurant, muttering indignantly. 'Miss Snooty-Toots, so far above the rest of us but can't make enough money in that hotshot little government job she's so proud of to pay her bills.'

His words were like throwing ice-water on already frozen bones. Sarah shivered and bent to pick up her coat, successfully hanging it on the stainless-steel hook this time.

When would she learn? She'd mastered ducking and shrugging and dodging, just like the rest of the female employees. When would she learn to master her mouth? Living in the nation's capital took two jobs. 'Maybe three,' she mumbled to herself, trying not to think about the fact that the gas company had turned off the heat in her apartment yesterday. She had to make enough in tips today to get them to turn it back on.

She nudged her way through the swinging doors that led from the storage-room to the kitchen, and reached into the box under the counter for one of the padded order forms. 'Hi, Chet,' she greeted the morning cook. She didn't wait for his answer as she hurried into the main part of the restaurant to take her place on the floor.

She'd worked as a waitress throughout high school and most of college, so smiling and refilling coffee-cups was second nature and Sarah automatically went about her business, still mentally berating herself. She couldn't afford to make Len or anyone else mad.

She was thankful that it was a hectic Saturday morning. Besides her having the chance to make great tips, Len would stay busy with the cash register and seating customers. He'd have little time for staring holes into her.

Kathy, one of the other waitresses on duty, materialized beside her. 'Shall I take coffee around for you? I've got a few minutes.'

Sarah felt her eyebrows raise in surprise. When Kathy wasn't busy she usually took smoke-breaks in the hall by the kitchen. 'Thanks,' she accepted, and watched with interest.

Of course. The man in the front booth explained Kathy's lack of interest in having a cigarette-break. Sarah had noted his good looks when she'd taken his order but that was all the admiration she'd had time for.

Intercepting one of Len's venomous looks, she turned on a smile and approached the back booth. She had just finished taking the elderly couple's order when Kathy returned and handed her the coffee-pot.

'Nice, huh?' Sarah commented on the customer.

'Yeah, but that was a waste of time and energy.' Kathy sighed. 'His nose is buried so deep in that paper, he never even noticed me.' She pouted in disappointment.

'Cheer up, Kathy. You can take him his next refill, too. Maybe you'll have better luck.'

'Forget it.' Kathy tossed her head, flipping her long dark braid. 'He's probably married and has ten kids. The classy ones always are.'

'He's too old for you anyway.' Kathy was barely eighteen. The man had to be in his mid-thirties, Sarah decided, admiring his straight dark hair and the mature broad shoulders.

The signal that an order was ready drowned Kathy's response. 'That's mine,' Sarah said, and moved toward the kitchen to pick up the order.

'It's *his*,' she teased Kathy as she swept by her a moment later on the way to the front booth. 'Maybe you'd like to write a message on it in butter? That might catch his eye.'

'I'll bet you his tip you don't fare any better,' Kathy said, heading back to her own section. 'You'd have to do something pretty drastic to get his attention.'

'Why would I want it?' she wondered under her breath, until the man raised electric-blue eyes. His polite smile contrasted with his mega-volt tan and dazzled her.

No wonder Kathy was interested. If he made her legs shaky without expending any effort, what could he do if he put his mind to it?

'Here you go.' She leaned to place his waffle in front of him just as a rambunctious child screamed past her like a whirlwind. The little boy clipped her in the knees from behind. Wavering precariously, she caught a glimpse of the tow-headed three- or four-year-old on his way to raid the Treasure Palace near the cash register. She watched in horror as a sculpted flower of melting butter took flight toward the man's shirt-front. She grabbed for the waffle. As if in slow motion the tiny pitcher of syrup tottered in the other direction. After that, everything happened quickly.

The waffle landed on top of the buttered silk shirt and left a trail of yellow behind as both slid down his chest. The thick plastic syrup container landed on the edge of the table, spouting like a whale's blowhole as it bounced, then thunked to the floor. Sarah did an awkward dance, first avoiding the flying syrup, then skating as it formed a pool beneath her feet. Her foot shot out from under her.

'Are you okay?' The man's words were out almost before she hit the floor.

'I'm not sure,' she gasped. Her breath was gone, but whether from being knocked out of her or from gazing into the man's blue eyes she wasn't sure. She mentally examined her various body-parts for pain. She didn't feel a thing.

'I wasn't serious,' Kathy said, rushing to her aid. 'I didn't mean anything *this* drastic.'

The man's eyes were wide, intense with concern. Kathy was right. Sarah definitely had his attention.

The corner of Sarah's mouth twitched, and she felt her cheek crease with her one lonely dimple. A self-conscious giggle grew in her throat.

Kathy hooked her fingers under Sarah's arms and tried to tug her up. 'You okay?' she asked, then lost her grip. Sarah slid back to the floor and her laughter really erupted.

'Let me help,' the handsome man offered.

He stood, and the waffle flipped from his lap to hers. He looked at her in amazement, then a conspiratorial grin replaced his surprise and they were both laughing.

With a sparkle in his eye, he extended his hand again. 'Come on.'

Her hand stuck to the floor when she tried to lift it. She shook her head. 'Not a good idea,' she said, drawing a deep breath, looking up at him. 'Not unless you want syrup all over you as well as all——'

'You incompetent idiot.' For the first time all morning Sarah had forgotten Len. His furious voice quickly reminded her that he was aching for a reason to pounce on her—in a fight he could win. Her heart sank with a dull thud. 'This is the last straw, you clumsy——'

'I'm afraid you don't understand,' the stranger broke in.

Len straightened; his tone turned pompously soothing. 'I am sorry about this, sir.' His beefy hands curved over the customer's shoulder reassuringly. 'Len Freiman. I'm the manager,' he said. 'Let me get you something to clean up with.'

He ordered Kathy off to get a clean damp cloth. 'And the cleaning bill is on us, of course.' He cast Sarah a nasty look and she had no doubt who the 'us' was. 'Rest assured, this incompetence will not go unpunished.'

'If you don't mind my saying so, Freiman——' the man's eyes turned frigid '—the young lady wasn't at fault. The child crashed into her. She—or the child—could have been seriously injured.'

'It wouldn't have happened if she had been paying attention.'

Tired of being discussed as if she weren't there, Sarah tried once again to pick herself up off the floor. A sharp pain arrowed through her ankle and she groaned.

The stranger immediately leaned over, disregarding both her employer and her concern about sharing the sticky mess. 'I've got the butter and the waffle; I might as well have the syrup, too.' He captured her hands before she could protest further, and lifted her until she was standing on one foot. Then, very gently, he eased her into the booth across from where he'd been sitting. 'Where does it hurt?'

'My ankle.' She studied the throbbing joint. 'I think I may have sprained it.'

'It's a ruse,' Len said.

A dangerous glint settled in the customer's eyes, leaving them as dark and cold as a stormy sky.

'Just another excuse for causing chaos,' Len said, ignoring the warning. 'You have customers waiting, Sarah.' Len's last few words rose in a surprised croak as the stranger turned on her boss and grasped the collar of his dingy white shirt.

'Are you finished?' Sarah saw the man's jaw clench, relax, then tighten again. 'If not, you'd better say your piece now. You haven't bothered to look at her ankle. You haven't expressed one reasonable sentiment of concern.'

Len sputtered.

The customer waved at the syrupy floor. 'And you might want to get this cleaned up before someone else gets hurt.' His hard-edged voice raised slightly. 'As

an attorney, I'll gladly represent anyone who chooses
to file a lawsuit if your continued negligence causes
further injury here.'

'It isn't like we've had——'

'And get her things.' The man waved in Sarah's
direction. 'She wouldn't continue to work for you if
her life depended on it.'

'Wai...' Sarah started to protest, then caught a
glimpse of Len as the man stepped aside to gaze down
at her. Len's jowls wobbled in a mixture of rage and
humiliation. His plump cheeks were the dark red of
an overripe apple. His bulging, stunned eyes and the
way his small mouth opened and then closed helplessly made him look like a fish out of water. And no
amount of soft talk was going to save this job, she
realized. She straightened her slumped shoulders as
Len's eyes narrowed hatefully. 'I'll pick up my check
next Wednesday.'

The stranger gave her a look of approval as Len
jerked around and stalked away.

The man watched until Len disappeared behind the
kitchen doors, then leaned over her again, blocking
out everything but the bright fluorescent light behind
him. The glow seemed to radiate from him.

A real-life knight in shining armor, she thought,
rescuing a damsel in distress. It wouldn't have surprised her to look past him and see a white charger
snorting impatiently.

'Shall we get you to a doctor? That ankle's starting
to swell.'

The reminder brought her back to reality with a
painful jolt. 'Just slightly,' she said, examining the
offending ankle again. 'I'm sure it will be okay.'

Kathy returned with the damp rag and handed it to him. He wiped his hands, then offered the cloth to Sarah. 'I don't think this is going to help our clothes,' he said, 'but you may feel a little better with some of it off your skin.'

'Here, Sarah. Len told me to clock you out.' Kathy handed Sarah her purse and jacket. 'You quit, huh?'

Sarah glanced up at her champion. 'It was quit or be fired,' she told Kathy quickly, easing some of the dismay that crossed his features as he realized what he had done.

They had drawn a huge audience. Eating had stopped and everyone in the place watched with interest.

Sarah thanked Kathy briefly for all her kindnesses.

'You too.' Kathy gave her a self-conscious hug. 'Now, if I were you, I'd get out of here before Len comes out with the mop and bucket.' She smiled viciously. 'The dish-washer never showed this morning, and he can't find anyone to stick this messy job with. He's furious.'

'Just what I need.' Sarah grinned, hooked her purse under her arm, and tentatively stood up.

'Don't worry,' the knight reassured her. 'He's not going to start anything.' He reached for his jacket from the other bench.

'Let me know what happens,' Kathy mouthed, rolling her eyes toward the man before he straightened and offered Sarah his elbow ceremoniously.

'We're out of here,' he said. He started to throw a dollar tip on the table, then looked from her to it. 'I guess this is yours.' He stuffed the bill in her pocket.

'You've done quite enough, thank you,' she said primly, taking his arm with as much dignity as she could muster.

The door to the outside closed behind them as they heard Len return with a clatter of metal and mop handles.

Sarah giggled like a kid playing hookey from school. 'Whew. I don't think my ex-boss is a happy camper.'

'I don't think so,' the man she leaned on agreed, then looked around the parking lot questioningly. 'Are you going to be able to drive?'

'Yes. I mean, no. I mean, I don't have a car,' she said hesitantly. 'Would you mind helping me to the bus-stop?'

'You can't take the bus.' His expression reflected his horror.

'I do every day.'

'Look at you.' His eyes followed his own instructions, and suddenly Sarah was very aware of what he saw. She didn't miss the subtly raised brow, the slight widening of his eyes as they viewed her, really seeing her for the first time. His eyes paused maybe a split-second longer than necessary on certain sticky parts as he looked her over from head to toe, then settled back on her lips. She forced herself not to chew them nervously.

She couldn't possibly look good, with her uniform glued to her with syrup and her ankle held at an awkward angle in front of her. But his interest was somehow indefinably approving. Her cheeks warmed again.

'Yeah, look at me,' she laughed. 'I wouldn't climb into *anyone's* car this way. Especially not yours.'

'Aside from a rather large spot of butter—which you know all about—what's wrong with me particularly?' He looked down at himself, spreading his hands. He possessed the most lovely smile, she decided as she watched it grow slowly, mischievously across his face, then spread to his eyes, making them dance like sunlight on a cool lake.

'I didn't mean it like that,' she protested.

He went on as if she hadn't spoken. 'If you disregard the fact that I just overstepped the bounds of propriety by quitting your job for you,' he said, 'I'm not really such a despicable character that no one would want to be seen with me.'

What an understatement. Few men carried themselves with such certain, confident grace. Add in the shoulders, the long legs——

'I meant I'd ruin your car. I couldn't do that to anyone, let alone the man who has rescued me from the big bad wolf.' Her hand gestured toward the restaurant. 'Your support in there . . .' She left the sentence unfinished. 'And as for the job, I would have been lucky to have lasted the rest of the day. Did you see his face? Believe me, Len was more upset because he wasn't going to get the chance to get back at me than he was about anything else.'

'What for?'

'It doesn't matter. You did what I should have done two days after I started here, and I'm grateful enough not to mess up your car.'

'My car will wash. And you're just too polite to tell me your mother told you not to accept rides with strangers.'

She laughed. 'Right.' But she knew the battle was lost as soon as he extended his hand.

'Mark Barrington,' he presented himself. 'And you are Sarah...?'

She frowned for a second, and then remembered that both Len and Kathy had said her name. 'Fields,' she supplied.

'See how easily we took care of the stranger problem?' he said, supporting her as he hopped her toward an elegant cream-colored car in the center of the lot. 'Let's get you to a doctor.'

'Home,' she corrected. 'I'm all right.'

'You're sure?'

She nodded. 'I will be as soon as I'm home.'

He looked skeptical. 'Okay, home, then.'

He installed her into the passenger seat of his car, only sticking to her once. 'You're a mess, Sarah Fields,' he said cheerfully as he climbed in the other side.

'So are you,' she said as he pried his fingers from the car keys.

'Now, where do you live?'

Sarah prattled mindlessly as Mark helped her up the first flight of stairs and finally picked her up and carried her up the last set to her third-floor apartment. She hoped her chatter would keep his mind off the less than attractive surroundings. From the look on his face, she was failing miserably.

She also hoped to distract herself from the feel of the arms that held her so carefully, yet casually. That wasn't working either. By the time he set her down outside her door to dig through her purse for her keys, she was a bit breathless—which was silly, since he was the one who had exerted himself.

'If you're going to sprain your ankle often you ought to find a ground-floor apartment,' he panted. In her wildest dreams she couldn't talk herself into believing that her maple-scented nearness had induced that effect on him.

'And in a different neighborhood,' he added as three dubious-looking youths stepped out on the landing below them. They wore the colors of one of the area's gangs, and paused to study Mark and Sarah speculatively.

She thanked him and opened the door. She would have slipped in, slamming it in his face, but he was quicker.

'What in heaven's name are you doing here?' he asked, looking around.

'I live here,' she said.

'But you're not from here. Your accent's too flat.'

'I'm from the midwest. Kansas. A little town about seventy miles from Wichita,' she added when he would have launched into another diatribe.

'And your mother knows you're here?'

'Of course.'

'I don't mean here, DC. I mean she knows *this* is where you're living?'

She lifted her nose a notch. 'She knows my address.'

Mark actually snorted. 'And you've invited her to visit soon, right? Didn't anyone warn you that you've moved into the middle of one of the most crime-ridden neighborhoods in the whole United States?'

'It's what I can afford,' she said quietly. She didn't need his critical assessment of her problems. They were hers; she was handling them. She didn't plan to be in this neighborhood forever. 'Would you prefer me homeless? I've seen a lot of those unfortunate people since I came here. And, frankly, I don't plan to join them.'

She hobbled toward the one piece of furniture in the small room with as much dignity as she could muster. Her ankle throbbed. The impact of losing her job had slapped her in the face as soon as they'd pulled up outside. Before too much longer she was going to cry. It was coming as surely as Mr Knight-in-Shining-Armor Barrington stood there gaping at her. She wanted him gone before it happened.

She painfully sidestepped him, and he followed her to the sofa. 'I'm sorry,' he said. 'I bit my tongue all the way up here and obviously quit too soon. I have absolutely no right to say a word about . . . about your lifestyle.'

She sniffed, and the first tear sneaked out between her lashes.

'Oh, Sarah.' He groaned and swung her up in his arms again, carrying her toward the couch. 'Oh, Sarah, please don't.'

'I'm trying not to,' she whispered against his neck. 'I didn't want to do this before you left.'

He nestled her down on the couch. 'You have to get that up,' he said gruffly, indicating her foot. 'And get some ice on it.' One side of the room opened into a small galley kitchen. He headed that way.

'Wait, Mark——'

He opened the refrigerator. It was too late. He leaned out around the door. 'Something seems to be wrong with your refrigerator,' he said.

She shook her head and slunk down full-length on the couch. 'No electricity,' she muttered, flinging her arm across her eyes. Good old Sarah Fields. Up to all her old tricks. When she humiliated herself, she did it right.

She heard him come halfway back. 'What?'

'No electricity,' she said again, enunciating carefully.

She didn't need to look at him to know that he was stunned speechless again.

'It's only been off since Wednesday.' Maybe if he knew it had only been a couple of days he would close his gaping mouth.

He recovered quickly. A muscle in his jaw twitched as he grabbed her one throw-pillow and tucked it beneath her ankle. 'We have to get ice on that. Where could I buy a bag?'

'Mark, there's no——'

'I'm not leaving until I've done that, at least.' His jaw was set in a hard square line.

She realized the futility of protesting. Maybe getting ice would soothe him enough to prevent him turning her into his own personal charity case. 'Mrs Byers—down on the first floor, left side—would lend you some. She's been really nice to me.'

He left without another word.

'Tell her it's for Sarah,' she called after him.

He looked grim when he finally returned. She didn't have the nerve to ask what had taken him so long.

'Where's your bathroom?'

She directed him and in minutes he reappeared, wrapping a towel around the plastic ice-bag. He braced it around the swollen ankle. That done, he sank down on the floor beside her. 'Have I seen the worst?'

She had managed to pull herself together in the time he'd been gone, and even had her story ready for when he asked. It was really none of his business. 'You've seen it.' Sarah offered him a tentative smile.

'The rent's paid?'

Why did he have to ask direct questions? She was lousy at lying. 'I'm only two weeks behind . . .'

He started to say something, but she interrupted. 'With today's tips, I'll have enough to catch up a week. I'll be able to convince the manager to let me stay.'

He swept a hand through his thick, dark hair. 'Sarah, you don't have today's tips,' he reminded her. 'I quit your job for you. Remember?'

She produced the dollar he'd stuffed in her pocket, trying to cheer him up. 'Yes, I do,' she laughed.

He scowled. 'You don't even have a job now, thanks to me.'

'Oh, but I do.' She seized the opportunity. 'That was my second job.'

'You're living this way with two jobs?'

'It's not that bad,' she protested. How could he judge her lifestyle so hastily? Someday *she* would have a car and wear expensively tailored shirts. 'I have a good job. I'm a research assistant with the Department of Education.' She felt the usual stirring of pride as the title flowed off her tongue. 'The job at the Pancake Palace was just to give me a little extra while I get on my feet.'

She saw him literally bite his tongue to keep from commenting.

Smart. The man was smart. She wasn't sure she could take another of his cynical remarks.

'Monday is payday again,' she assured him. 'I'll be okay. And I'm slowly but surely getting myself out of the hole I got myself into when I first got here.'

'How long ago was that?' he asked.

'Not quite four months.' She answered his next question before he could ask it. 'I just didn't realize how high the cost of living was here. And I'm looking for a roommate. That will help.'

'But no one in their right mind will move to this neighborhood.'

'I'll find someone soon,' she said.

'And in the meantime you can't pay your utility bills.'

'Which is why I had a second job.'

He blanched.

'I'm sorry,' she apologized instantly. 'I appreciate your standing up for me. It was the most chivalrous thing anyone has ever done for me.'

'Fools rush in ...' A sheepish grin softened his face as he let the old adage hang, unfinished.

'How could you know my predicament?' She suddenly laughed. 'And the look on Len's face will get me by until long after I find something else to take the place of that horrible job.'

'And in the meantime? You can't even go look for another one.'

'This is a temporary setback. I'll figure out something,' she said quickly as he reached for his back pocket. 'And I won't take your money.'

'Well, at least let me give you today's tips.' He withdrew a bill—she couldn't see its denomination—from the wallet he'd opened.

'No, please, Mark. I can't accept——'

'How much?' he asked. 'What do you generally bring home in tips?'

'You're with the IRS, right?'

He didn't even smile.

'What about your parents? Could you get a little from them to tide you over?'

She stiffened slightly.

'Wouldn't they help you?'

She craned her neck to look out the bare window at the nothingness in the concrete courtyard below. 'Of course.'

'But you won't ask.'

'Right.' She closed the subject with pursed lips. He didn't need to know that she had over-enthusiastically contributed half her paychecks to getting her brother into college before she'd realized just how high her own expenses would be. Her mother was so proud of her—the first college graduate in the family—and thought she was doing very well. How could she stop sending money home now?

'Do you mind if I give you a little bit of advice, Sarah?' he finally asked.

'Probably.' She met his eyes reluctantly, sure that he was going to say whatever it was whether she minded or not.

'Go home,' he said gently. 'This isn't Oz. There aren't any wizards here. Go back to Kansas. You aren't ready for this.'

His words hurt, probably because he'd spoken aloud her biggest fear. 'I won't be in an entry-level position forever. I plan to move up. In another two months I'll get a raise.'

'If you survive that long,' he said on an exasperated release of air.

'It's not your worry.'

'It wasn't till I quit your job for you,' he said impatiently, placing the bill he'd taken from his wallet on the box that she'd been using as an end-table. He glanced at his watch and jammed his fists in the pockets of his neatly pleated slacks. 'I have someplace I was supposed to be an hour and a half ago,' he said, his blue eyes burning into her hazel ones. 'Is there anything else I can do before I go?'

'No,' she said, avoiding his eyes. 'I can't think of a thing, Mark.' She extended her hand. 'You've done more than enough already. Thanks.'

He winced. 'Don't remind me.' His hand closed around hers and her fingers tingled with the touch. His grip tightened momentarily.

'What about work Monday? How are you going to get there?'

'Oh, I'm sure——'

'I'll pick you up. What time do you have to be there?' he interrupted.

'That's not necess——'

'Humor me? You know, play along, just to make me feel better? It'll do wonders for my guilt.'

His obvious frustration with her problems charmed yet saddened her. Before he'd seen all this everything had been so warm between them. 'Okay. I would very much appreciate a ride to work Monday,' she agreed softly. 'But please, Mark, believe me. That job was a lost cause long before you stepped in.' She wondered if telling him about Len's inappropriate advances would make him feel better. Probably not.

'I've never been rescued by a knight in shining armor before. It was very——' She started to say 'romantic' and blushed furiously. 'It was every woman's dream come true.'

He glanced down at his shirt. 'I'm afraid the armor is a little tarnished.' He sighed. 'And the tarnished knight absolutely *has* to go.' He removed his wallet again and she started to protest, but he plunked a business card down on to the table beside the money. 'You call me if you need anything,' he ordered.

She nodded, convinced he wouldn't leave if she didn't.

'Promise?'

'I promise.'

'Then I'll see you later.'

'Monday morning? Seven-fifteen ought to do it,' she said.

'Later,' he corrected, opening the door. He hesitated, making leaving look like hard work. When he finally closed the door, it was with a decisive thump. Then his hand reappeared around the edge and he twisted the lock before snapping it shut again.

Sarah waited for the sound of his steps on the uncarpeted stairs. It came. Finally. She sighed in relief. She definitely had enough problems without complicating them with a man. Especially one who could get under her skin rather quickly if she wasn't careful.

CHAPTER TWO

DAMN! The word became a litany with each stair Mark stomped down. How could he go and just leave her here? Not an ounce of food in that useless refrigerator, her ankle swollen to the size of a grapefruit and a landlord ready to kick her out. Where would she go?

He briefly wondered if he should find the manager, catch up her rent, since he was certain that she wouldn't accept money personally. She'd be furious.

It was an option he could consider later, he decided. 'You've got plenty of your own problems right now,' he muttered, glancing again at his watch. He left the stuffy atmosphere of the building and emerged into the filtered light of the dew-heavy morning.

He rounded the corner, headed for the pot-holed parking lot. A group of youths stood evaluating his car. 'Hey!' His shout didn't disturb them in the least.

They looked up, almost as a unit, watched him coolly for a second as he broke stride, then resumed their perusal of the BMW.

'Nice day,' he commented, keeping his voice casual as he neared them.

One, the obvious leader since the others looked to him for a reaction, nodded toward the car. 'Yours?'

'Yeah.' Mark took the keychain from his pocket and stepped around the boy nearest the hood to get to the driver's side.

The leader jerked his head, silently commanding the gang to join him on the sidewalk. 'Bad,' he commented.

'Thanks,' Mark said. He glanced up, locating the window in the line across the top of the building that he thought was Sarah's.

'Thirty-three B? She your lady?' the leader asked, his interest piqued.

'He was with her,' one of them commented, and Mark recognized him as one of the boys he and Sarah had seen on the landing earlier.

No, dammit, she isn't my 'lady' but you leave her alone. His hand tightened around his keys. 'I'm working on it,' he said. Maybe verbally staking a claim would dampen their obvious enthusiasm for her. Good grief, what she was doing here?

His territorial feelings were downright primitive. He briefly considered going right back in there and dragging her—kicking and screaming if he had to—from the building that sat like a hideous growth on the landscape. He wanted her somewhere safe. Away from here.

The next image that popped into his head was a little less noble.

Getting in and starting the car, he lifted his hand to the motley-looking group and set the car in motion.

He found it almost unconscionable to drive away. He couldn't even comfort himself with the knowledge that she'd been coping before he'd interfered. She'd obviously been hovering on the brink of disaster since she'd arrived in DC.

Mark pulled into a strip shopping center near the hospital and went into a small men's store. He bought an off-the-rack knit shirt to replace the butter-stained one. However ill his father was this morning, he *would* notice if Mark appeared wearing his breakfast.

Breakfast. His stomach growled as he changed in the rest room of the convenience store next door to the clothing store. Trashing the ruined shirt, he stopped at the counter and bought a candy bar. Couldn't be much worse than a waffle smothered in butter and syrup, he thought as he popped the last bite of chocolate-covered nut and caramel into his mouth, then licked his fingers. But candy for breakfast left him with the same sense of impropriety that he had felt leaving Sarah back in those apartments.

She was helpless, her shapely leg propped on a pillow and her naïveté as prominent as the ponytail she wore high on the back of her head. He was sure the boys in wherever-she-was-from, Kansas wouldn't have left her at the whim of a bunch of street toughs that made references to her with obscene gestures. He impatiently pushed his thoughts of her aside and drove the last couple of blocks to the hospital.

He had intended to be here by nine, about the time his father's latest chemotherapy treatment would be finished. If past experience was anything to go by, his father would be ready for a little comfort. He hoped this session had been better.

False hope, Mark thought as he stepped into the room. Reggie Barrington was ashen. In some indefinable way he seemed beaten, ancient.

'Dad?'

His father's eyes opened wearily.

'Sorry, Dad,' he apologized. 'I meant to be here sooner.'

The corner of Reggie's mouth turned up slightly. 'I'm glad you missed the worst of it.'

Mark slumped down on the arm of the chair beside the bed and took his father's hand. It felt dry and papery. 'If this is what it takes to make you well, Dad, then it's worth it.'

Reggie's soft chuckle started a spasm of retching. When the episode ended he added wryly, 'That sounds like something I told you when you skinned both knees learning to ride your bike. I guess I deserve to get back my old platitudes.'

'I knew it sounded familiar.' Mark spooned a chunk of ice from the cup on the stand. 'Here, this will help.'

'Thanks.' Reggie raised his head to accept the cool sliver, then eased back into his pillow.

The circles beneath his father's eyes were deeper, sunken, almost bruised-looking. 'It was worse this time?'

'It's probably just my mood.' The older man's blue eyes, a faded version of his son's, fixed on Mark. 'The news isn't good, Mark.'

Mark's body stilled. 'The tests yesterday?'

Reggie nodded. 'Dr Hartlie said we're not making much progress. Said the damned disease is gaining ground faster than we are.'

Mark cleared his throat and straightened. 'That's why you're feeling down, Dad.' It was a statement. 'You're not giving up?'

Reggie's look came close to its usual sharpness. 'You know me better than that.'

Of course, thought Mark. Silly assumption where his father was concerned. The man was as tenacious as a bulldog.

'But the prognosis was a bit disheartening.'

'What exactly did Hartlie say?' Mark had to force the question out. He wasn't sure he wanted to hear the answer.

'Maybe six months. At this rate, six months if I'm lucky.'

Mark felt as if he'd been punched in the stomach. The denial and sense of helplessness he'd experienced when his father had told him he had Hodgkin's disease overwhelmed him now. He barely resisted folding over in a tight ball. Damn! He should have been here. How dared Hartlie give his father bad news when no one was here to take the edge off it?

Reggie patted Mark's hand. 'I'm glad you weren't here,' he said, as if he knew what Mark was thinking. 'It's given me time to think about what's important to me, Mark. I'm ready to go, if that's how it works out.'

'You can't think like that, Dad. It sounds as if you *have* given up.'

'I haven't,' Reggie assured him. 'Hartlie said there's still a chance the chemo might work. There's no reason to give up hope. Or treatment.'

'Good.'

'But I'm a realist. It's time to face the possibilities and I've been lying here thinking about those and taking stock.'

The lump in Mark's throat wouldn't let him speak even if he could think of something to say.

'I've been thinking about your mother,' Reggie went on. 'You know what kept me going after she died, don't you?'

Mark shook his head.

'You. I wanted to go with her. Marcella was every-thing I lived for once I finally found her, but I had to stay and raise you, see you grown. She would have never forgiven me for not putting you before my own pain. But you're grown now, and I'm very proud of you.'

'Dad——'

'That makes the thought of dying easier,' Reggie went on, as if Mark hadn't interrupted. 'But I quit mourning her long ago. I've put all my effort into enjoying you. And I've been selfish. Letting us live like two bachelors with little thought past doing whatever we wanted to do. Now I'm not sure you re-member what it was like to be part of a real family.' He grimaced with another spasm of pain.

Mark grabbed his hand and held on for dear life.

'Sorry,' Reggie said wearily once it was over.

Mark offered him another piece of chipped ice and swallowed the lump that blocked his throat. How could the man think of himself as selfish when he apologized for his own pain?

'Do you remember much about your mother, Mark?' Reggie asked. 'We were so happy, the three of us.'

Mark suddenly remembered Sarah. *That* was who she had reminded him of. Not in looks—Marcella Barrington had been dark and dramatic-looking, and except for his father's blue eyes and commanding physique Mark was his mother's son. Sarah was fair, with golden-brown hair the color of Kansas wheat, hazel eyes that sparkled like sunlight on a rippling lake. But she'd sat there laughing in a pool of syrup and summoned up memories of his mother. 'My strongest memories are of her laughing,' Mark said.

'Mine, too,' Reggie agreed. 'The joy we shared is what I thought about after my talk with Dr Hartlie this morning. What are you going to have to keep you going when—if,' he revised as Mark started to protest, 'I'm gone?'

'I've got my career, Dad, and...' Mark stumbled.

'And?' Reggie prompted. 'Meting out justice isn't going to keep you very warm at night.'

'And friends. And Millie.'

'What friends, son? You didn't name a one. Mark, I want you to have someone you love and care enough about to share your life with, especially the laughter. I want you to have what I had with Marcella. If you were happily settled, married to someone who could make your life as complete as Marcella and you have made mine, I'd have no qualms... about joining her. Life's been good.' He brushed moisture from the corner of his eye and the lump in Mark's throat grew so big that he thought he'd choke on it.

'I've always assumed you'd find someone eventually. And when I thought at all about it, I thought I would live to see you married, sharing everything with someone you love. With maybe a few kids of your own. I can't bear the thought of you not having what we had. And I can't stand knowing I won't have time to enjoy your happiness.'

'You've never said anything before, Dad.'

'I didn't have any reason to.'

'I *have* met someone, Dad.' The words dropped out of Mark's mouth unexpectedly. Reggie's eyes lit so eagerly for a moment that Mark wouldn't have taken back the impulsive words if he could. Consciously, he added fuel to the fire. 'And it wouldn't surprise me if she was the "one".'

Reggie actually eased himself up on one elbow. 'Really?'

'Yeah. I haven't been able to quit thinking about her since we met.'

'I was afraid I'd turned you into a self-sufficient bachelor. I didn't know you were looking.'

'I wasn't. Things have just sort of happened.' Oh, this was good medicine. Reggie's face glowed with enthusiasm.

'That's how it happens,' Reggie assured him. 'The right woman comes out of nowhere and takes you by surprise. Who, Mark?'

'Her name's Sarah. She works for the Department of Education. She's from Kansas.'

'Where did you meet her?' Reggie pumped.

'In a restaurant. We shared breakfast one morning.' Mark grinned. So far he hadn't told one untruth— maybe an exaggeration or two—but he'd had the butter, she'd had the syrup. Couldn't share breakfast much more than that, could you?

'So why haven't *I* met her?' Reggie demanded. 'Why haven't you brought her home with you?'

'I haven't known her long.' He looked down at his long fingers, studied the neatly manicured nails. 'And I don't have any idea how she feels about me.' Probably pretty irritated now that she's had time to think about my quitting that job for her.

'Can *I* meet her?'

Mark sighed. 'Let me work on it.'

'I'm not rushing you, Mark—these things take time—but you are thirty-three. And well-established. It's time you thought about settling down.'

'Sure, Dad. I can see that you have no intention of rushing me.' His father's smile made Mark feel as if he had just taken a happiness pill.

'Well, knowing you're at least thinking along those lines helps a little, but I don't have time for you to dilly-dally around.' Reggie gave him a wry look, but couldn't help adding with the same kind of friendly persuasion he'd been practicing and perfecting his whole life, 'And you don't have any excuses anymore.'

'She might.' Mark gently applied the brakes to the conversation. 'Don't you think she'll want some say in the matter, Dad?' he teased.

'You're darn good-looking, if I do say so myself. We've been beating off the girls since you were eleven. And you're a judge, a diplomat's son. And I saw how persuasive you could be when you were practicing law. So the question comes down to your deciding how much you want her.'

Pretty badly, Dad. If the thought of my finding a wife puts that kind of smile on your face, I want her a lot.

'With you sick, I've pushed any serious ideas I've had aside. The time didn't seem right,' he said deliberately. 'So I didn't realize until just now how seriously I *have* been thinking about her.'

'Well, just keep thinking along those lines, son, because believe me, the time is right.'

Sarah woke from her aspirin-induced sleep. She didn't know if her discomfort came from hunger-pangs or the chill. Either way, lying in a house with no heat and her leg wrapped in a towel soaked with melted ice wasn't very restful.

What should she do now? she wondered, preferring sleep. At least when she was asleep she couldn't think about her predicament. There was very little food in the house—she'd planned to eat all her meals this weekend at the restaurant. And when she'd gone to take a bath and clean up her ankle had hurt like the dickens. She knew she couldn't make it down the stairs and then the two blocks she'd have to walk to the store just yet.

She had expected Mrs Byers to be up to get the life history of the 'nice young man' as soon as Mark left. The woman made it her business to know everyone else's. She reminded Sarah of old Mrs Perkins back home. Both would have felt mistreated if anyone had kept something from them.

But Mrs Byers hadn't appeared. Come to think of it, the bag Mark had carried in had looked like one of those you'd buy from a machine.

She frowned. Mrs Byers had been her one and only hope of getting through the next two days. She thought of Mark's card. It was still lying where he'd left it. At the time it had amused her that it hadn't occurred to him that she might not have a phone. It wasn't very humorous anymore.

What if Mrs Byers didn't know there was a scoop and so didn't come up to find out about it?

Someone knocked and Sarah sat up, smiling. *Finally.* She knew she could count on curiosity. 'Come in,' she responded eagerly.

'The door's locked,' a masculine voice called, rattling the handle.

He'd locked it, hadn't he? 'Just a minute.' She unwrapped the dripping packet from her ankle and limped to the door. 'I didn't expect you back again today.' She tried to mask her relief at seeing *anyone*.

Mark took a deep breath. 'Actually, I need your help. And I may have the solution to your problems, too.'

Of course. When he'd left, looking guilty as sin, she should have known he would be back with some invented reason to force his charity on her. She knew how this worked. Sarah balanced herself on one foot, looking up at him sceptically. 'Oh? And what is that?'

'My dad is very sick right now——' he put a finger against her lips as she opened her mouth to offer her sympathy '—and he wants to see me married—well, happily settled was the way he put it—more than anything in the world, and I would do *anything* to make that wish come true.' He took a deep breath. 'How would you like to marry me?'

Sarah burst out laughing. Surely he didn't feel *that* guilty. She wobbled and he put both hands on her waist to steady her.

He grinned. 'I didn't explain that very well, did I?'

She shook her head. 'Not if you mean exactly what you said. It sounds like an extreme way to solve problems.'

He started over. 'I hope we can agree to an arrangement that would benefit us both, one that would make my father very happy.' His cleared his throat. 'I've laid the groundwork.'

'How?'

'When he brought the subject up you popped to mind, and I told him I thought I'd met the woman I wanted to marry. I said I hadn't known you very long and wasn't sure how you felt about me and he swallowed it whole. He only knew my mother for two weeks before they were married, so he accepted it without question. The only thing he asked me to do was to please speed things along a bit. Everything fell into place perfectly,' he added.

'But we couldn't get mar——'

'I wasn't proposing that.' His arm slipped around her waist and he started hopping her toward the couch. 'But I could take you to meet him. All you would have to do would be to play along. Act as if you're interested in me—as if maybe you're even falling in love with me. That wouldn't be so tough, would it?' He sat down, easing her down beside him.

No, she had to admit, acting as if she was falling in love with him wouldn't be difficult at all. Especially right now, with his eyes warm with excitement and his jaw squared in determination. Caring? Nice? And terrific looks besides? It was a heady combination. She could easily love someone like him.

'Then maybe in a couple of months or so—we would time things according to how he's doing—we could announce our engagement, throw a couple of parties to keep it all real for him, set a date, let the papers announ——'

'Oh, no. That would be taking it too far,' she said, drawing away from him a bit. His touch did strange things to her, made it hard to concentrate.

'He's got to believe that my life is set if...' Mark stumbled again.

Sarah automatically reached for his hand.

'I want him to see that he has nothing left to worry about as far as I'm concerned,' he explained. 'Will you help me put his mind at ease?'

'He's going to know, Mark——' she started.

'I'll chance it.' He waited for her answer.

Things were moving too fast. 'We've got to think this through,' she said slowly. 'If you're that close to your father, he wouldn't be fooled by something fake,' she pointed out.

'In other circumstances I'd agree, but he taught me years ago that half of convincing someone of something depends on their desire to believe. He has a personal stake in believing.'

Sarah saw the truth of that bit of wisdom when she realized she wanted to believe him. Against her better judgement, she wanted to help. She ordered herself to think logically.

Who was this man? She could be getting herself into something she couldn't handle. He might not even have a father.

And in the big city people apparently played all sorts of con-games with each other. Except for easing some of the guilt he felt, what could Mark gain from this? Glancing around her, she couldn't think of a thing.

And as she was analyzing the situation he was obviously reassessing her, too. He examined her from the top of her head to the tips of her toes.

She was a mess. She'd released her hair from the ponytail she'd worn to work. She'd donned a faded sweatsuit. She had nothing to offer him. She knew that any second now he would come to his senses and take back his wild suggestion.

But she felt the awareness that had been between them as he'd carried her up the stairs increase tenfold. Her skin grew too uncomfortably tight for her body. Maybe that was what he wanted. What else did she have to offer? But in a million years she couldn't imagine the man sitting beside her having to resort to this sort of game to get anything he wanted. She only had to remember Kathy's reaction——

'Your only obligation would be a kiss now and then,' Mark assured her, as if reading her mind. 'Small things to further the picture of the happy couple we want to present in front of Dad.'

His perception was very unsettling. 'Wouldn't your father be more likely to believe this if you were to ask someone closer to you to help, a friend you've known a bit longer?'

'Not for a second,' he replied bluntly. 'I've known them all too long to convince him that I'd suddenly fallen in love with one of them.' He stood suddenly and paced. 'Besides, do you know any other Sarah from Kansas who works for the Department of Education? I've told him that much.'

He sauntered in front of her, glancing around, scowling.

How could he ever believe that someone like her could fit into his world? 'Oh, Mark, you'd better ask someone else.'

'Who?' He stopped circling the room and examined the toe of his immaculately polished shoe critically. 'The others—the ones he doesn't know—they'd be too busy trying to turn the whole thing into reality,' he said slowly. 'I'd be busy trying to keep them at a distance. As you said, he's too perceptive.'

'How do you know I wouldn't do the same thing?'

'I don't,' he said after a moment. 'But I'm pretty good at reading people. I'm staking my father's happiness on being right about you.'

It was a quiet compliment, one she couldn't think of a reply to.

'Besides, your reactions in this aren't nearly as important as mine.' He withdrew the compliment as unwittingly as he'd given it. 'Dad doesn't know you. He doesn't have any preconceived ideas about how you *should* act.'

'I suppose that's true.'

'And that's what is so perfect about this whole scheme,' he said. 'We both have something to gain. You'd have every reason to want Dad to believe us.'

Had she missed something? Her mind raced back over the conversation.

He finally sat down beside her again. His hip brushed her leg, then remained warm against her thigh. She felt a pleasant electricity seeping through her from the point of contact. Her mind went in a million directions. None of them had anything to do with the subject under discussion.

He misinterpreted her blank look. 'I'm sorry, Sarah. I had everything lined out so clearly in my mind on the way over here, I expected you to understand automatically what I was talking about. I'm offering you a *job*. One that will take the place of the one I quit for you. I plan to *pay* you for your part in all of this.'

'Of course,' she said aloud. She'd been feeling flattered, as if she'd made a friend, as if he was asking

for her help because he thought of her that way. It
was all guilt.

She raised her chin slightly, and her ankle began to
throb again. The fifty-dollar bill she'd stuffed down
her bra for lack of a better place to put it prickled
against her skin.

'I wouldn't ask you to do this without gaining
something for yourself,' he said.

Convincing someone who wanted to be convinced
was easy. Wasn't that what he had said? 'And you
won't have to feel guilty anymore about my other job.'
She supposed someone like Mark could afford expensive guilt-trips.

She forced the closest thing to a sophisticated laugh
that she could manage from her tight throat. 'I can
recognize charity when I see it. And I don't want
yours, Mark Barrington.'

He gazed at her, perplexed for a moment, then
stood and swooped her up into his arms in one
motion. 'I guess I'll have to show you,' he said.

'Put me down,' she finally got out as he plunked
the purse she'd left by the door on to her abdomen.

'When we get to the car,' he said.

'Please, Mark, look at me,' she said desperately.
'I've still got syrup in my hair.'

'You've changed clothes.' He sniffed her neck. 'And
taken a bath. You don't smell like a smoky coffee-
shop anymore. And your hair's fine.'

'Can I at least get some shoes?'

He sat her down and picked her slip-ons up from
beside the couch.

'You need to go to the hospital anyway. The swelling
hasn't gone down a bit,' he said, watching her try to

stuff her foot into the shoe. 'I should have *insisted* on taking you to get an X-ray this morning.' He lifted her into his arms again. 'And what's a more believable excuse for meeting my father than a trip to the hospital because of an accident you had?' he added, continuing down the stairs.

She made one last attempt at a protest when he plunked her down outside the passenger-side door of his car and searched his pocket for the keys.

'But I can't afford——'

'I assure you the Pancake Palace has workers' compensation.' He unlocked her door, then pulled her against him and out of the way so that he could open it. 'And you have insurance through the other job, don't you?' He gently installed her in the seat, hovering over her until she looked up into his eyes. They held a bit of amusement and something else she couldn't define.

'But won't I have to pay up front?'

He nodded. 'Sometimes. If they insist, I'll take care of it,' he said equitably. 'Then you'll owe me.' He grinned and shrugged a shoulder. 'And right now I would love having you obligated to me instead of the other way around. Our account could become very unbalanced.'

He watched as she opened and then shut her mouth. 'Good. Save your breath,' he said. Unnecessarily.

What with the look in his eyes, the feel of his body against hers, the excitement rising in her chest—excitement for a job that would get her back on her feet, she told herself sternly—she couldn't have breathed right now if her life had depended on it.

CHAPTER THREE

ALMOST two hours later, at the hospital where Mark's father was, the emergency-room doctor confirmed that Sarah's injury was a sprain, wrapped it and told her to stay off it for a few days.

Sarah could feel her ankle throbbing a cadence that kept time with her nervous heart as they watched the numbers in the elevator steadily climb. The fact that Mark had grown more and more silent as time had passed didn't help.

'Mark, you aren't sure this is such a good idea anymore, are you?' she asked hesitantly.

'No.' He pushed the wheelchair that the emergency staff had loaned them off the elevator at the fifth floor and swung in front of her. He braced himself on the arm-rests of the chair and crouched in front of her, searching her face. 'The idea itself, maybe, but I'm not sure about you. I just realized I can't take you to see my father if you aren't going to agree to carry this through,' he said reluctantly. 'I don't think he'll take all this seriously if I introduce him to you then have to come up with some other Sarah-from-Kansas-who-works-in-the DOE.'

'Mark, I——'

'And I know I promised you could meet him and then decide, but it's impossible. You'll have to trust me.' His intense gaze pleaded with her. 'I will find someone else to help me if you won't,' he added.

She looked down at her hands. Her knuckles were white against the dark arms of the chair.

'I shouldn't have given him so many details——' his voice softened '—but I'm not sure I would have even thought of this if I hadn't just met you.'

She sucked in a long breath.

'Do you want this job or not?' His words emphasized that it was a business transaction.

Her heart flip-flopped, and for a second she wondered if that might not be the toughest part. She wasn't sure that she would always remember that it was *just* a job. As hard as she tried, she couldn't avoid his eyes. They bored into some secret place inside her.

'Let me do it as your friend,' she begged impulsively.

He frowned and shook his head. 'You need the money. I need the help. Doing it this way will keep it from getting messy.'

Messy, how? She might decide to hold him to his bargain? Blackmail him? Try to sue him for breach of contract if he reneged on his 'promise' to marry her? 'You have to trust me too,' she said.

He grinned. 'Okay, you caught me,' he admitted. 'I confess. I need to feel as if I'm the boss. After everything I've seen today I have a feeling you have an independent nature.'

She laughed. 'You caught me.' She used his words. How many times had her mother told her that she would be a lot better off if she showed the sense God gave her at least half as much as she showed her independence?

'Hiring an actress would cost me,' Mark said. 'And that is all this is. An acting job. This part was made for you. You won't *have* to act.'

What? Had he already realized how attracted she was to him? How much he fascinated her?

'All you have to do is be you,' he finished.

'And act as if I'm in love with you,' she murmured wryly.

'Tough assignment, I know,' he said cockily.

He definitely had enough confidence for the both of them. And he possessed an over-abundance of charm. It didn't seem fair.

'Okay, Mark, I want the job.' She couldn't afford to think about it any more.

'Good.' He looked smug. 'Let's go meet my dad.'

Mark paused outside a door that she was positive he shouldn't open.

'Wait.'

A fierce look of determination squared his jaw as he impatiently circled the awkward chair and sank in front of her again.

'Shouldn't we match our stories or something?' How could she do a job if she didn't have a description? Her eyes searched his face.

'Probably,' he agreed. 'But we'll be more likely to carry this off if we stick as close to the truth as we can and play the rest by ear. Dad's sick, not senile.'

She lifted her chin.

'Just pretend you like me—a lot,' he added for good measure.

'But I've never been good——'

'You've never been good?' He twitched his eyebrows up and down devilishly. 'Sounds promising.'

She ignored him. 'At hiding my feelings or play-acting. My teachers always said my face is like a mirror.'

'And you don't think you can act the least bit interested in me?'

She felt herself flush. What woman in her right mind wouldn't be interested in him? It galled her only slightly that he knew it. 'It's not that, but——'

His lips cut off speech, touching hers as lightly as the flutter of a butterfly's wing. His mouth lifted after just a second.

'I won't have any trouble convincing him I'm attracted to *you*.' Huskiness replaced the cynicism in his voice. 'Did you find that distasteful?'

She couldn't have answered if her life had depended on it. Shock robbed her of any air. Swimming sensations clouded her brain and made her head feel so light that she was certain it would float right off her shoulders.

He lowered his mouth against hers once more. This time his lips parted, and hers followed suit.

Her heart battered furiously against her ribcage. One of his hands cradled the back of her neck and sent wonderful sensations down her spine. She melted, weaker and weaker, into the sagging strip of cloth that held her.

She almost groaned when he finally lifted his head. It took a sheer force of will to bring her head back to an upright position and to focus her eyes on him. She felt as if she had just landed in the middle of a fairy-tale. She wasn't sure who she was, but he was definitely the handsome prince.

Someone behind him cleared her throat.

Sarah's gaze jerked to the nurse standing on the other side of the open door. A man in the bed behind the woman was almost breaking his neck, leaning forward to examine her from the top of her head to the bundled foot propped on the foot-rest of the wheelchair.

'Ah! Mark. Are you two going to stay out there doing that all evening? Or will you bring your friend in to meet me?' The old man's eyes sparkled as Sarah's face grew hot.

'Do we have a choice?' Mark sent Sarah a promising look. And even though she knew the 'promise' was for the benefit of their audience, the pace of her heart—which had stopped momentarily—picked up again.

The nurse turned sideways and slipped past, watching Mark with a definite air of disappointment. 'Why are the good ones always taken?' she sighed aloud.

Mark's father chuckled. 'And it's about damn time.'

Mark bent to whisper in her ear as he pushed her forward into the room. 'The element of surprise works every time. You look bemused and Dad is *convinced*. This is going to be one of the easier things you've done today. Just go along with me,' he added.

'Hi, Dad,' he called to the pasty-faced man impatiently pushing the button near his hand. The head of the bed rose with a mechanical hum.

'I want you to meet Sarah Fields,' Mark said. 'Sarah, my dad, Reginald Barrington.'

'Reggie,' he modified for her. 'You didn't have to tackle her to get her to agree to come, did you?' Reggie stared pointedly at her bandage.

'A little kid tackled her this morning.' Mark wheeled her closer to the bed and she offered Reggie her hand. 'I thought I might have to tackle her to get her in here to have her ankle checked, though.'

She expected a handshake. Instead, Reggie bent and kissed her fingertips almost reverently. Then he grinned as if he had just found a pot of gold in his own backyard. 'She blushes. It's charming. I can't tell you how pleased I am to meet you, Ms Fields,' he added. His grip grew tighter the longer he held her hand.

'It's nice meeting you,' she mumbled, still so embarrassed that she felt tongue-tied and silly. She glanced up at Mark with a blatant plea for help.

'We can't stay but a minute, Dad. Sarah's had the kind of day no one should have more than once a lifetime.'

Reggie's bushy white brows almost met over his nose as he scowled in concern. 'But some of it has been good, surely?' he asked hopefully.

She lifted one shoulder. 'Sometimes a bad day makes you more appreciative of the good ones.'

Reggie laughed. 'Another diplomat in the...'

She saw Mark shake his head in a nearly imperceptible warning to his father.

'Well, every day can't be perfect.' Reggie tried unsuccessfully to hide his disappointment.

'But good things sometimes come from bad. If Sarah hadn't sprained her ankle, we wouldn't be here,' Mark pointed out. 'And, since we were, I thought I might as well run her up here to meet you.'

'Meeting you has brightened my day considerably,' Sarah added.

Reggie chuckled. 'See. A diplomat,' he said to Mark.

'And we promised them in the emergency-room that we'd bring the wheelchair back right away,' Mark said. 'Since the nurse in charge reminded me of Aunt Rhonda, I don't think we'd better press our luck.' Mark stepped between her and the bed and touched his father's hand in a way that did everything a long hug could have. Sarah felt suddenly homesick at the tender but not obvious display of affection.

Mark turned back to her. 'Now, let's get you home, Sarah, and up all those stairs.'

Reggie directed his concern at her again. 'Where do you live?'

'In a third-floor apartment with no elevator,' Mark answered before she could open her mouth. 'Now, let's get this wheelchair back before that Aunt Rhonda prototype comes looking for us.' Mark winked at his dad. 'See you in a little while.'

'Don't come back tonight, son,' Reggie said as Mark steered Sarah around the end of the bed. 'Sarah could probably use another bright spot or two. You two go out and eat or something.'

'You're sure, Dad? You wouldn't like the company?'

'Positive.' He started lowering his bed. 'I'm tired and you've got work to do.'

Mark frowned.

'The project we discussed this morning,' Reggie reminded him.

Sarah felt her face go pink again. She hoped she didn't give away the game. Obviously Mark had decided that now wasn't the appropriate time to tell his father their 'good' news, but that didn't keep Reggie from pushing.

'I'd appreciate it if you would work on that tonight. I'll be asleep in five minutes,' Reggie added.

'Okay, Pop.' Mark shook his head. 'See you tomorrow, then.'

'It was nice meeting you, Mr Barrington.'

'Reggie,' he corrected. 'And you take care of that ankle, Sarah.'

'Later,' Mark promised Reggie, and pushed her out into the hall.

Neither of them spoke until they were at the elevator again. 'That wasn't so bad, was it?'

Sarah breathed a silent sigh of relief. 'No. I like your dad,' she added.

'Even if he's a little impatient?' he said with humor.

'Why didn't you tell him? I thought that was the whole point.'

'If we rush it too much he won't be as likely to believe.' He punched the 'down' button.

The doors slid open and they shared the elevator with three other people going down.

'I take it you didn't want your dad knowing where I live,' she commented when the last of the strangers got off at the lobby. They continued on to the lower-level emergency entrance.

'I was saving you a lot of trouble.'

'He wouldn't approve of me if he knew?' she asked.

'Nothing like that,' he corrected. 'But he would have had you moved out and in with us in the next hour. That was where he was headed anyway. Didn't you see him light up when you said you lived upstairs? He looked triumphantly at your bandaged foot and was getting ready to offer to send a moving van.' His lips formed an analytical line. 'I didn't think you'd appreciate his tactics,' he added.

'Why?'

'Yeah, I guess I should educate you about the way he works.' Mark released a wry chuckle. 'You have to keep in mind that Dad spent his life fine-tuning the art of diplomacy.'

'And that means?'

'That he's one heck of a manipulator,' he said.

'Like this situation,' Sarah said, the light dawning. 'He manipulated you into asking me to...into initiating this farce.'

'Not quite.'

She frowned up at him.

'He didn't know about you or even suspect that I might be interested in matrimony right now—with anyone.' He looked smug momentarily. 'I took a tiny bit of information he gave me and used it against *him* this time.'

'But I thought this was for his benefit.'

'It is.' He grinned. 'Lesson one: ultimately, a master manipulator—excuse me, I mean diplomat—must *believe* he's doing what he is doing solely for the benefit of the one he wants to manipulate.'

'Oh.'

'We *are* doing this for his benefit. And he wants to believe it more than anything—an element of lesson two,' he said in an aside as the nurse he had called an Aunt Rhonda prototype came toward them. 'It ought to be easy if we don't let him trap us into anything we don't want to do.'

She looked up at Mark, watched him interact with the nurse, and wished she could start the day over again, back at the Pancake Palace.

The pay wasn't exactly great, the work wasn't especially satisfying and the boss wasn't nice by any definition. But at least she had known what to expect. Right now she was totally confused.

She had the feeling that she had fallen headlong into a den of con-artists who would steal her independence. And convince her that she liked it in the process.

Out of the frying-pan, smack into the fire. As much as she liked both Mr Barrington and Mark, she had the sneaking feeling that she was going to have to be very, very careful.

'So explain lesson two,' she said as Mark helped her into the car a few minutes later.

'People can only be manipulated if they want to be.'

'I didn't want to be tricked into moving into your house, so how would your father have manipulated me?' Another thought struck her. 'And you told him I lived in a third-floor apartment with no elevator. Wasn't that playing directly into his hands?'

Her naïveté obviously amused him. 'It's the only way you can win.'

'He wouldn't...couldn't have convinced me to come stay with you. Besides, why would he?'

'He decided I needed help since I didn't have you signed, sealed and officially engaged to me in the four hours since I last saw him.' He eyed her in a heart-stopping way. 'Dad knows me well. He took one look at us and figured close proximity and the chemistry between us would finish us off.'

Her hands fluttered nervously until she folded them together in her lap. 'I could have held my own with him.'

'No way.' He laughed. 'He would have won.' He pulled up in front of a quiet but very nice restaurant. 'Let's go eat.'

'You've got to be kidding. I'm not going anywhere like this.'

'That's what you said before we went to the hospital.' Mark climbed out and came around to her side of the car. 'The people who manage this place aren't going to think a thing about the way you look.'

'They may not, but I do. I'm not going in, Mark.'

He looked at her for a moment, evaluating her again. 'You are stubborn.'

She nodded and folded her arms around her waist. 'Meeting your father like this was bad enough. And you know these people? Whatever reputation you have, you won't have any of it left if you insist on taking me around looking like this—especially if you intend to announce that we're engaged.'

'I heard your stomach growling way back when we were waiting for the results of the X-rays. You can't make me believe you're not hungry.'

'Maybe not,' she semi-agreed. 'But if you insist, why don't we drive through somewhere and get chicken or something to go?' she suggested.

Mark threw up his hands in mock-exasperation, closed her door and went to his own side of the car. A few minutes later they were sitting beside a fast-food drive-through window, waiting for the order he had placed without even asking her what she wanted—twice as much as they both could eat in three evenings. And my refrigerator doesn't work, so I can't save it for later, she thought ruefully.

For once, the thought didn't make her feel desperate. She'd be able to pay the electricity bill as soon as Mark paid her.

'You're always this stubborn?'

She nodded.

'Then I have a feeling I need to explain to you the nature of employee and employer.'

'That *and* free lessons in avoiding being manipulated?' She rolled her eyes dramatically. 'You should describe all these additional benefits right up front, and then you wouldn't have to work so hard at getting prospective employees to take the job you're tying to fill.'

His head went back as he let loose a delighted, full-blown laugh. He was making it very difficult to keep in mind that it was a job, that he was her employer, that they weren't just friends helping each other out.

'And for all those valuable benefits I should get at least an amenable employee,' he said finally. 'And maybe I underestimated you.' He raised one brow speculatively. 'Maybe you'll give my dad his greatest challenge.'

She could tell that he liked that idea. 'Are *you* always like *this*?'

'Like what?'

'Manipulative.'

This time he chuckled quietly. He had a very nice laugh, though it sounded a little rusty. He obviously hadn't used it much lately.

The young boy manning the window handed out Mark's change and a huge box containing their order. Mark placed the box between them and drove on.

Sarah had not yet become accustomed to the contrasts throughout the area surrounding the nation's capital. There would be several blocks of stately mansions, with lush, carefully tended lawns and gardens, followed by areas with small houses and apartment buildings practically crammed on top of each other. Then there were other, unique neighborhoods, made so partially by the small stores with signs in different languages and displays of interesting and sometimes horrifyingly mysterious items.

She usually roared above or below everything on the city's very efficient public transportation system. She'd been so impressed by it that she had sold her rickety old car within weeks of moving here.

Of course, the natives didn't agree with her assessment of the system, and griped constantly about it. They'd never lived miles from anything except a grocery store and a post office. She found it all very liberating.

Too many times, she'd been bound by a low fuel tank or a battery that refused to hold a charge anymore or a blizzard that didn't stop for days.

But this *was* nice, because Mark was the one coping with the city traffic and the confusing circular layout of streets. And she enjoyed seeing the city from the hushed atmosphere of his luxurious car.

'Here we are,' he said, pulling into an empty slot across the street from her building. 'Let me get you in, then I'll come back for the chicken.'

'I can walk.' She moved quickly to step out on her good leg before he could get around the car. 'Let me lean on you and I'll manage.'

He reached in for the food and pushed the automatic locks, then offered her his arm.

Ten minutes later they were only halfway up the second flight of stairs. 'I should have let Dad have a go at you. This isn't working.' Mark set down the box and started to pick her up.

She nodded at the chicken. 'That won't be here by the time you get back,' she warned him, and her stomach growled for emphasis. 'I'm all right. Just let me rest for a minute.' She leaned against the bare railing.

'Give me your keys,' he ordered.

She complied.

'I'll put this in your apartment and be right back.'

She watched him run up the stairs, then renewed her efforts. She had only made a couple more steps on her own when he returned.

'Hang on,' he said, plowing into her mid-section like a linebacker. 'We're going to starve to death and the food will be inedible by the time you make it upstairs on your own.' He braced her across his shoulder like a bag of flour, and set her down inside her door a minute later.

'Sit down here.' He eased her toward the couch. 'And tell me where the plates and utensils are.'

She gave him directions and he went to bang around the kitchen as she slid to one end of the couch and stretched her aching leg out full-length. That left just enough room at the opposite end for him. She leaned back against the arm.

What a day! she thought, glad that it was almost at an end. The light outside was fading. A few crickets had started their evening song.

She sighed wearily. She'd known him now for about twelve hours and for most of that time she hadn't known which end was up.

When he wanted, he turned on the charm. She had the sneaking suspicion that if she wasn't careful she would be following him anywhere, anytime.

Never mind that he was bossy and manipulative and obviously spoiled rotten. He was ... just Mark, she guessed, not coming up with any appropriate description right away. All she really knew about him was the little bit of background he had given her on their way to the hospital.

He'd lived all over the world while his father was assigned with the diplomatic corps. Reggie had retired from that when Mark reached high school age, so that Mark could spend his formative years in the States. Mark was a graduate of Georgetown University and had been, until recently, a practicing attorney. Just six months before—about the time that his father had found out about the cancer—Mark had been appointed a judge in the District Court. He hoped eventually to move up in the judicial system.

How far? she wondered. The Supreme Court? She had her own dreams and ambitions, but nothing as daunting as the highest court in the land. The memory of the kind of investigation and interrogation they did into the background of one of those candidates gave her a shiver. Mark was obviously also nuts, she decided.

The breeze coming in through the open window was cool. She rose on her good knee to close it, and movement across the street, near where Mark had parked, caught her eye.

It took a second for what she was seeing to sink in. The thugs that haunted the neighborhood were 'working' on Mark's car, she realized. And she had no doubt that when they were done it would never be the same.

'Stop that,' she yelled out the gap in the window. 'Get away from that car!'

One of them looked around, shrugged, and returned his attention to whatever he had been doing before she'd hollered. The others never even slowed down.

'Get away from that car,' she yelled again, louder. 'I've called the police. They'll be here any time now.'

That caught their attention. This time, the 'work' stopped, and one of them pointed toward her apartment. The other six youths looked up, following the line of his finger.

'What in heaven's name are you doing?' Mark's voice snapped, so taut and close to her ear that she thought he would take it off. 'My God!' he exclaimed as he realized what was going on. With that, he turned and ran out of her apartment. She heard him clunking down the stairs, a minimum of two or three at a time.

She turned to stare back at the scene below. Her relief at the reduced size of the group was short-lived. Something glinted in the glare of one of the recently lit streetlights, and her heart stopped as she realized that the remaining three boys wielded switchblades now.

Two of them slashed maliciously at Mark's tires while the other semi-crouched with his back to them, standing guard. He screeched an obscenity up at her.

Mark! Terror clutched her throat, keeping the scream jammed inside. Even if she could have got it out, she knew he probably couldn't and wouldn't hear the warning. Helplessness settled over her like a stone.

The thugs turned suddenly toward the front of the building. She snapped her eyes shut. She just couldn't watch.

Sirens sounded a few blocks away and for an instant Sarah almost believed she *had* called the police. It took her a second to remember that she couldn't have without a phone. She'd never wished more desperately for anything.

She peeked again. Mark stood alone beside his car, hands on his hips.

She carefully inspected every inch of the area around him and saw no sign of the vandals. She didn't know she'd been holding her breath until it escaped in a loud sigh.

Mark spun, looked up directly at her, paused for a long moment, then strode toward the building.

She heard him on the stairs long before she saw him, and from the heavy, dreadful sound of his footsteps she wasn't surprised when he came in shouting furiously.

'Damn it, Sarah. Do you have any idea what you've done? Even the vaguest, remotest idea?'

She could only look at him wide-eyed. Her mouth gaped, but not one word came.

'Do you know those boys?'

This time at least her head moved.

'That's what I was afraid of,' he said between clenched teeth. 'You can't identify any of them.'

'I've seen them around. I could identify a couple of them, maybe.' She shook her head again. 'But it was too dark. They were too far away.' At his look of total exasperation, she grimaced.

He paced to the door, slammed it, then walked wearily to the couch. He sank down beside her on the edge as if his long legs wouldn't support his strong body any longer. She scrunched away from him, telling herself that she was giving him room, and he dropped his head into one hand and raked through his hair with his long, splayed fingers.

'They'll be back,' he said. 'You know that, don't you?' He finally looked sideways and over his shoulder at her, waiting for her response.

'They're neighborhood kids. Of course they'll be back. But I...I don't really think...I...'

'You don't think you have anything to worry about?' he asked her softly. 'Guess again.'

She gazed at him wordlessly. She was so relieved that he was all right, that he hadn't come to any harm, that moisture clouded her vision. Her lip quivered for a second.

'If you could identify them by name we could go right down to the police station, have them picked up.'

'I'm sure I could point out a couple of them if I saw again. One of them lives in this building.'

'You surely don't believe they're just going to come into the police station so you can pick them out of a line-up, do you? *No one* could be that naïve.'

'Of course not,' she said defensively.

'And if you could, you'd only be safe for a day or two because of their previous records—I'll bet all of them have records three miles long. They'd be released eventually and out for blood. And they'd hold you—not their own vandalism—responsible.'

'Then it's a good thing I didn't call the police,' she said brightly.

'You just *said* you did.'

'So. Nothing happened. They'll forget it by tomorrow.'

'No way. Eventually you're going to pay. You can't stay here now. You know that, don't you?'

She'd watched too much TV, too many movies not to suspect that he might be right. The good guy-bad guy, edge-of-your-seat suspense shows were her favorite. That didn't mean she wanted to star in her own real-life version of one. She laughed shakily.

'I'm glad you see something humorous about this.' The corners of that sexy, magical mouth turned slightly upward.

She took a deep breath and gradually transformed her mild hysteria into spastic hiccups. 'It's funny, Mark,' she said finally. 'You have to admit, from beginning to end, this whole day has been crazy. And there are days when laughing is the only thing that gets you through it.'

He raised one brow skeptically and shook his head. 'I'm glad you can,' he said quietly. 'And you *do* still have syrup in your hair.' He softly tugged on a glued-together strand, then smoothed it back in place.

For a moment his eyes lingered on her lips, and she thought he was going to kiss her again. The thought changed to a wish.

Instead he stood up, swung her legs out and eased them to the floor. He extended his hand. 'I'm going to help you to your room. You're going to pack a bag while I find a phone and call the police, and my auto club... and a cab to take us home,' he added as an afterthought.

She looked at his long, shapely fingers, sighing, knowing that he was right. She couldn't stay here.

'Could we eat first?' she asked.

This time *he* laughed. 'You're kidding?'

'No. I'm starving.'

'It's ready. I guess we may as well eat it, but I can promise that the chicken is going to be cold. It was barely warm a while ago.' He hesitantly headed for the kitchen. 'If we took it with us, Millie could heat it in the microwave.'

'If we take the bare bones when we leave, we can throw them at those thugs if they have the nerve to mess with us again.' Her stomach protested loudly.

'Maybe we should go now; your growling stomach would scare off an army.' He shook his head in disbelief. 'How long did you say you'd been here?'

'Four months.'

'It's rather difficult to think of you as lucky,' he said, 'but nothing else explains what has kept you off the list of murder and rape victims in the district. It sure as hell hasn't been street-smarts.'

She tilted her chin slightly. 'I'm learning.'

Something in his eyes reluctantly agreed with her. 'I just hope to God you learn fast,' he replied. 'I can't stand the thought of you learning the hard way.' He cupped her chin in his hand for a moment, studying her as intently as possible in the tiny amount of light left in the dark room. 'Maybe that's why all this is happening. So you won't have to learn by yourself.'

'So you can help me?'

'So we can help each other,' he said softly, then went to get the chicken and some candles.

CHAPTER FOUR

SARAH'S eyes widened as their taxi pulled up in front of a high fence much, much later. Mark withdrew a small gadget from his pocket and pushed several numbered buttons. The ornate gates blocking their way glided quietly open.

Night and the huge trees scattered over the park-like grounds blocked any view of the house, but Sarah had the sinking feeling that it was going to be more impressive than she could imagine.

Granted, the neighborhood she'd just come from wasn't what she was used to either, but for most of her life she'd shared a poverty similar to theirs. And poverty was poverty. The effects were just more noticeable in this huge city than they were in small-town middle America. And the tracks separating the 'haves' from the 'have nots' weren't as visibly uncrossable.

In Elmwood the 'haves' went to the same schools as the 'have nots', they shopped at the same grocery stores, knew the same people. The differences mostly depended on the kind of house you walked into each night, the cars you did or didn't drive, and on what you did on hot Kansas summer nights.

When the air had been so thick that it was hard to breathe, let alone sleep, her middle-class friends had been home in their beds, soaking up central air-conditioning, while the kids from the poorer section of town were sneaking out in the middle of the night, meeting at the park and occasionally stealing sodas from the machine they'd learned to jimmy at the corner gas station.

She knew from experience that the good folk from Elmwood considered it all as negatively as the people from here saw their gangs. But in comparison the kids from Elmwood were harmless.

Sarah couldn't think of those nights without thinking of Sean Cole. The thought wasn't a comforting one, since Mark Barrington reminded her of Sean in a lot of ways. She glanced at Mark, saw his eyes focused on her in the dimly lit car, and quickly looked away.

The house—make that mansion—slid into view as they rounded a gentle curve in the long drive.

Sarah felt panicky. She was definitely out of her element. If she hadn't fitted in the neighborhood she had just left, she certainly didn't fit here.

Mark's hand covered hers. 'It's a lot less formal than it looks,' he said. 'In fact, Millie gets quite irritated because she thinks Dad and I treat the old "ancestral" home too irreverently.'

Sarah shivered. Mark's hand tightened on hers. Its warmth felt reassuring.

'I should have insisted you wear your coat,' he commented as the driver stopped in front of the massive front door of the three-story structure. He paid the fare, giving the man a generous tip, if his rush to get her bag out of the trunk was any indication. Mark asked the driver to carry it to the house, and bent to pick up Sarah.

'I can——'

'I know,' Mark said impatiently, 'but this will be much quicker.'

The front door opened and a plump, white-haired woman peered out. 'That you, Mark?'

'Yes, Millie. Did you get the room ready?' He strode toward the house easily, despite her weight.

'Sure did,' Millie said. 'And I just got a call from the hospital.'

Mark halted in his tracks. His arms tightened around her and his heart thrummed hard against hers.

'Nothing's wrong, hon,' Millie assured him. 'Mister said the doctor told him he could come home in the morning. So—you know him—he decided he might as well come tonight. He wanted you to pick him up.'

Mark deposited Sarah next to her bag on the marble floor inside the huge foyer and introduced her as a friend. Millie accepted Sarah's extended hand and frowned at the bundled foot.

Mark cut the niceties short. 'I'll let you help Sarah get settled and I'll get to the hospital.' He scowled. 'I guess I'll have to take *my* car.'

'Just stay put.' Millie stopped him. 'He should be here any time now. I told him you weren't home yet, and he said he'd call a cab.'

'But——'

'Don't stew,' Millie ordered. 'He'll be much more comfortable in a cab than he would be in that little toy thing you call a car.' She looked at Sarah a little more appraisingly. 'Maybe now you'll get something a little more sensible,' she added smugly.

'By sensible I assume you mean something that will hold carseats and babies?' Mark laughed. 'Reggie must have mentioned that I brought Sarah by to see him.'

Sarah felt herself flush as Millie looked from Mark to her. 'It isn't such a horrible idea!' she exclaimed indignantly, planting her fist on her nearly non-existent waistline.

'Well, between you and Reggie, you're going to scare her off.'

Sarah cleared her throat. 'Only if everyone keeps talking about me as if I'm not here.'

The dry comment earned a chuckle of admiration from the housekeeper. 'And it's a good thing you are,' Millie told her adamantly. 'What in heaven's name were you doing in that part of town?'

'I live there,' Sarah said, and wished she hadn't.

Millie's eyebrows raised several inches in surprise, then her eyes sharpened on Mark. 'Mister certainly wasn't pleased you went and got the BMW tires slashed there.'

Mark grinned. 'I didn't do it.'

'It wouldn't have happened——'

'Come on, Millie. We can't keep Sarah standing around like a flamingo all night. Let's get you settled before Dad gets here.' He turned to Sarah. She sagged gratefully. 'I didn't mean to cause all this tr——'

'It's no trouble.' Millie waved the protest away and picked up Sarah's suitcase. 'I don't have enough to keep me busy as it is. In the old days Mister's mother and father kept it full of people and parties.' Millie started up the stairs. 'Now, half the time *they* don't even eat at home.' She shook her head uncompre-hendingly. Mark stepped toward Sarah, one brow lifted as if expecting her refusal of help. She hobbled the two or three feet between her and the first step.

'Which room did you put her in?' he called to Millie, who was two-thirds up the stairs and still muttering.

'The rose one. I was going to put her in the downstairs guest room, but with Mister coming...'

She didn't need to finish the statement. Mr Barrington needed to be downstairs so that Millie could care for him.

'Let me,' he said, close to Sarah's ear.

'I can——'

'I know, slowpoke, but it will be much easier to get you settled in if we do it before Dad gets here.'

She nodded reluctantly, bracing herself for the feel of his arms around her again. He hefted her up, turning her slightly so that she faced him. 'You're light as a feather, you know. Millie's going to want to fatten you up a bit.'

She eyed him skeptically.

'She will,' he assured her. 'She can't help it. Millie has a protective streak as wide as the sky. The only problem you might have with Millie is that she'll be watching to make sure you don't want to marry me for my money. You wouldn't be the first,' he added arrogantly.

Sarah's giggle burst from her like air gushing from a punctured balloon. 'You've just capsulized our whole agreement.'

'But it was the other way around. My idea. I want something from you. And I'm willing to pay to get it.'

They paused at the top of the stairs while Mark shifted her weight in his arms. She felt him watching the color climb in her cheeks as her breasts pushed more solidly against his chest. She licked her lower lip nervously.

The movement caught his gaze.

She squirmed in his arms. 'I can walk from here,' she insisted.

He put her down, holding her against him to steady her. She could feel every hard angle of his body.

'Such an innocent, virginal blush,' he commented. 'You surely aren't a virgin?' The heat of the word grazed her cheek and blended with the heat already there.

'I don't see how that is any of your business,' she said breathlessly. 'I agreed to be your fiancée, not your lover. So . . . so . . .'

'For everyone concerned—especially my father— the two have to be synonymous.'

She nodded and stared at the top button on his shirt, then started to turn away. She hesitated a fraction of a second too long.

His grip tightened, drawing her even nearer, if that was possible. She stilled immediately. If she moved a fraction of an inch she would meld with him, to the point where she wouldn't be sure where she left off and he began. Even breathing seemed to stoke the fire leaping to life in her bones.

'You aren't totally averse to the idea.' The back of his forefinger stroked up the side of her neck and came to rest behind her ear. 'I can feel your heart—here— and your pulse is racing almost as fast as mine.'

'Exertion,' she said. 'All this hobbling around takes its toll.'

'I was hoping you were reacting to me,' he said as matter-of-factly as he might discuss whether it might snow. 'Being lovers would heighten the illusion we want to create. And nothing says we can't enjoy this while we make Dad happy. We're two mature adults with nothing to lose.'

That helped her find her voice. 'I don't play with fire,' she said primly. 'Throwing sex in would only complicate things. You're paying me to do a job; sex wasn't part of the job description. And if that's what you want, maybe you'd better go look on the street corners downtown.' She broke out of his embrace and spun away, too quickly. Her weakened ankle almost didn't hold her. If he hadn't grabbed her she would have fallen.

'I didn't mean——'

'I know. But it's a bad idea,' she interrupted, shrugging away his hands. She knew she was over-reacting. And he was right—she was very attracted to him. A simple touch made her blood bubble and speed through her veins.

'Sarah.' For the first time since they'd met he looked flustered, and her stomach flip-flopped again. 'I keep forgetting that you're——' He broke off abruptly.

'That I'm what?'

'That you're a bit naïve,' he said reluctantly, pointedly looking past her, ignoring the angry snap in her eyes.

'Probably too naïve to carry this off. I think you'd better take me back to my apartment.'

'Calling you naïve isn't an insult, Sarah. If anything, it's a compliment. It's just that most of the women I see——' He took a deep breath and amended his statement. 'A lot of the women I meet are sophisticated...' His finger touched her mouth to delay her interruption. 'And worldly. It isn't that unusual to take a woman to dinner then casually take her to bed. In college, and until the complications of the past several years, it was almost expected.'

His voice softened. 'And in my mind I carried you up the stairs and flashed on the movie *Gone With the Wind*.' He grinned. 'I remember Rhett Butler sweeping up the stairs with Scarlett O'Hara in his arms. What man wouldn't love to see himself as some great romantic hero? And which one——' he lowered his voice to a whisper '—wouldn't love to put the glow on your face that Scarlett had on hers the next time we saw her? I'm sorry. I was fascinated by the idea.' His eyes were warm and bright and sincere. But they still smoldered with desire.

His eyebrows rose quizzically. His half-smile charmed her, and begged her to forgive. Sarah had to suppress a shiver, and stiffened her spine to keep from melting at his feet. She wanted to sound as calm and cool as he did. The only way she could do that was if she didn't say anything at all.

Then the doorbell rang and saved her as Mark glanced over the banister. 'Millie went down the back stairs about the time we came up these,' he explained. 'I hope she gets it.'

'That's probably your father,' she offered. 'You'd better go. I can make it from here.'

He shook his head. 'Dad would have them bring him to the back and come in through the garage.' He scowled. 'It's probably the tow truck with the car.'

When no footsteps were forthcoming she said again, 'Go. I'll be fine.'

'You're sure?'

'Positive.'

He paused halfway down the stairs. 'Sarah?'

She had limped part of the way toward the room he had indicated but was still clutching the railing. She leaned over questioningly.

'Thanks.' He gave her a thumbs-up gesture.

'You're welcome. I think.'

Mark grinned. 'And that last? That was lesson three.'

'Lesson three?'

He nodded. 'Dad taught me that it never hurts to ask if you want something.' He let his eyes tell her exactly what he wanted. 'If you don't ask, you certainly don't get.' He shook his head. 'And sometimes I amaze even myself with how well I learned all his lessons.'

'Two against one? I think that means I'm *really* in trouble.' She couldn't believe she'd said her thoughts aloud.

'You're right. It is two against one.' He winked. 'But that's you and me. We're in this together. Remember?' he reminded her. 'And you don't strike me as the type who can be easily manipulated—I've been trying all day now—so I don't think you're going to have any problem.' He turned and loped the rest of the way downstairs, chuckling to himself.

* * *

Sarah sat on the bed, after unpacking the meager belongings she had brought, staring at the cheerful floral and striped wallpaper.

She had heard them all rushing about downstairs so she knew that Reggie was home and settled. Did Reggie know she was here? Lord only knew what Mark would tell him.

So much had happened in the last fifteen hours that she felt as if she had lived a lifetime in one day.

She shook her head to clear it. So here she was, set to play the part of his fiancée, but she felt like a pampered prisoner in an ivory tower. She'd been stashed here and left to...to do what? To wait until it was time for her to go on stage? And then what would she do? She was a lousy actress. An even lousier liar. He'd chosen the wrong performer. And she felt so alone. 'We're in this together', huh?

So where was he? She released a sigh of pure frustration and sank back against the headboard, hugging the knee of her good leg to the pillow cradled against her chest.

'Sarah?'

She would have known it was Mark without looking or hearing his voice. He was the only person she'd ever met who could cause a tingling sensation to dance around her body by just staring at her.

He poked his head inside the room. Lines of concern furrowed his forehead.

'Yeah?'

He approached the bed slowly. 'May I come in?'

She smiled. 'I left the door open, hoping you'd come back eventually.'

He sank down beside her, tipping the mattress in his direction. She balanced herself so that she wouldn't roll into him. 'You don't like the room?' he asked after a moment.

'What's not to like?'

He looked around. 'I know people who really hate French Provincial furnishings.'

'I didn't even know that was what it was called.' She felt the corner of her mouth turn down.

'I don't think that's a major problem.' He stretched himself full-length beside her and propped his head on his fist, looking up at her.

'I told Dad I'd asked you to marry me.'

'And what did he say?' She felt as if her life hinged on his words.

'He asked if you'd said yes.'

She urged him to go on with her eyes.

'I said you had.'

'Why?' she asked, horrified.

'Because you did agree.' He smiled, his blue eyes gleaming mischievously.

'You shouldn't have told him!' She hugged the pillow she held tighter.

'Cold feet?'

She nodded.

He bounded up and spun to close the door. He leaned against it for a second before he started toward her again. 'You want to tell me about it?'

'Oh, Mark, look at this...' Her hand waved vaguely at the room in general.

'What? You can't do this if you don't know the proper name for the style of furniture?'

'It's not the furniture.' Her tone was strident and she forced herself to soften it. 'It's everything, Mark. How are we going to fool anyone when we don't even know each other? If it were just the style of furniture, I could handle it. You shouldn't have brought me here. I'm going to mess this up before we even start.'

He raised one eyebrow, asking if she was finished.

She wasn't. 'What do I know about you? I don't even know...' Shoot! The choices were mind-boggling. She knew nothing! She chose one. 'I don't even know what kind of music you like.'

He sat down on the side of the bed and pulled the pillow she cradled away from her. Casting it aside, he imprisoned her hands. 'So ask me anything.'

Suddenly her mind was blank.

'My favorite kinds of music are soft rock, classic, bluegrass and jazz. But I like almost anything.'

She scowled. 'Oh, that's vaguely helpful.'

'I know,' he acknowledged. 'We just don't have time for silly games.'

She twisted her wrists from his grip. 'Anyone with eyes will see that we don't know a single thing about each other. This whole scheme is doomed.'

'You can know that in two hours?'

She nodded, but the movement became hesitant under his intense scrutiny.

'Two hours?' he asked again incredulously.

She couldn't do more than sigh and throw up her hands in exasperation. 'I'm out of my league,' she said wearily. 'I had such high hopes about coming here. I don't mean here to your house,' she hurried to explain as he started to interrupt. She desperately sought understanding in his eyes. 'I mean here to Washington, DC.'

His sympathetic look didn't help her concentration. 'Whatever I do, I just keep getting further and further out of my depth. If I can't handle everything else, how am I going to handle this? I think maybe you were right this afternoon. Maybe I should just go home, before I mess everything up for you too.'

'Sarah,' he admonished her gently. 'After everything you've gone through so far, you're going to give in to self-pity now?'

She hung her head.

'At least I know you're human now,' he continued. 'I was beginning to wonder, since you seem to smile through everything.'

She met his eyes and fought tears. 'You were right about my parents,' she admitted.

He quirked one brow.

'I've let them think I live in a wonderful—but small—apartment and that life is just hunky-dory. My mom would have a fit if she saw the way I was living. I wanted to do this on my own so desperately.'

'What makes you think you aren't?'

'You had to rescue me.'

'It looks to me as if you rescued me. And my dad.' He was suddenly on his knees beside her. 'And what we know about each other's past isn't nearly so important as what we do in the future.' He lifted her chin with one finger. 'That's why this is so perfect, Sarah.' His hands drifted down to her shoulders and stayed there. 'I like you. I *want* to know you better. To help you. I said you should go home before I saw Dad. And I knew the minute he started talking about my getting married that you were the perfect answer to my problem, just as I'm the answer to yours.'

'But what are we doing? Hopping right out of the frying-pan into the fire?'

He shook his head adamantly. 'No.' Sinking back on his heels, he reached into the pocket of the faded jeans he'd put on sometime in the past hour and a half. 'Everything is falling into place perfectly. I even have an engagement ring for you.' He withdrew a simple diamond ring from the snug pocket. He blew on it and rubbed it on the knit shirt he'd had on since he'd returned to her apartment earlier.

'It needs cleaning, probably the setting double-checked. But I bet it fits. Want to try it?' He reached for her hand, but she was hesitant. 'I'll make a deal with you.' His eyes challenged her. 'We'll take this as a sign—good or bad. If it doesn't fit, we'll call the whole thing off.'

He waited for her nod of agreement.

She held her breath as he grabbed her finger and pushed it on. 'See? Fate is taking care of us. I knew it.'

He wouldn't have struck her as the fanciful type in a million years. But first Rhett Butler, now this? 'You believe in Fate?'

'Sometimes. Things happen that don't make sense with any other explanation.'

'Like today?'

'Like today,' he assured her. 'Even the stuff with the car.' He grinned momentarily. 'Not that van-dalism isn't likely enough if you park your car in that neighborhood,' he added with a cocky grin. 'I wanted to bring you here the minute I saw that apartment.'

She stared at her finger. 'Where did you get this on such short notice?'

'From Dad. It was Mom's,' he said. 'Dad said you might want something of your own; he assured me he wouldn't be upset if that was the case. It's a bit old-fashioned.'

'It's beautiful. Simple and beautiful.' A shiver of apprehension shook her. 'But now I feel worse than ever.'

He didn't even pretend to understand.

'Your dad gave this to your mother for all the right reasons. Now I feel as if we're making a mockery of their marriage.'

He lowered his head. 'Dad won't know,' he said thoughtfully after a moment. 'And he'll be ecstatic if you wear her ring. That's everything—the only thing—I care about right now.' His jaw was suddenly very square, very hard and determined. 'We will make this work.'

The ring was still warm from his body-heat, and as she adjusted the position of the stone she felt it branding her, binding her tight to the promise she'd made outside Reggie Barrington's hospital door—for money. 'I just wish my motives were as pure as yours,' she sighed. 'This would be ten times easier if it weren't for the money. Are you sure you won't let me do this just because I want to?' A weight of guilt slumped her shoulders.

'Money's the best motivator I know,' he said wryly. She glanced up quickly, and caught a bitter twist in his smile. 'Without it, what incentive would you have to keep up the act if the going gets tough?'

She wanted to say, Because I want to, but knew he'd see it for what it was: a pretty flimsy reason. Especially given that they'd known each other all of a day now.

'And I don't know why *you're* worried about messing up, anyway,' he continued. 'It will be much harder for me than you.' His tone relaxed and held a teasing note that eased some of the tension between them.

'Oh?'

'Of course it will. He knows me better than he knows you,' he said. 'He'll spot any discrepancies immediately if I don't act appropriately.'

'Just don't say I didn't warn you. If I try to lie, it's as obvious as the nose on my face,' she retorted.

'I don't know about you, but I can't see the nose on my face unless I look in a mirror.'

'Then you haven't tried like this?' She crossed her eyes and looked down.

He laughed.

She loved it. Knowing she had caused it warmed a spot in her heart.

'Sarah, we've gotten much too serious lately. Even if we weren't engaged you're exactly what Dad and I both need around here. I have a feeling you're going to be great medicine for him. That will make it easy for him to believe I would love you.'

He quickly filled her in on the mundane things that she would need to know in the morning. 'And now I'd better let you get to bed.' He leaned over to give her a peck on the cheek and then stood. 'See you in the morning. You'll be fine, hon.'

The speed of her heart picked up momentarily, until she remembered that Millie had laced her speech liberally with the endearment. It didn't mean anything. Mark probably used it out of habit. She groaned and buried her face in the pillow.

Mark had eased every qualm—except one. She was going to have to remind herself constantly not to get carried away by their own scam. How was she going to convince everyone that this was genuine without getting caught up in the fantasy herself? And Mark falling for her? That was definitely one fantasy she couldn't afford to believe.

CHAPTER FIVE

SUNDAY morning breakfast, Mark had said, was an informal affair, with everyone helping themselves from the spread Millie laid. Giving her directions to the dining-room, he had finished his instructions last night by saying that Sarah was welcome to sleep as late as she wanted.

She made her way downstairs slowly the next morning, pleased to be getting around better than she had the day before. The heavy wrap on her ankle and the long soak in the luxurious tub in the bathroom attached to her room had helped immensely.

Being warm, snug and secure all night hadn't hurt either, she admitted. And her worries now were a different kind; they lacked the sense of desperation.

Reggie sat in the chair at the end of the long table, casually sipping coffee and reading the paper.

'Good morning, Sarah,' he called. She hesitated by the door, surprised to see him. She waved him back down into his chair but he disregarded the motion. He almost glowed as he approached her.

'I'm so glad you're here.' He gently took her arm and escorted her to the chair next to the one he had occupied.

'I'm glad you're here, too,' she said. 'You look greatly improved since yesterday,' she complimented, partly for something to say, partly because he really did. His lightly tanned face had been a pasty mask yesterday. Today, the pallor beneath the tan wouldn't be noticeable at all if she wasn't looking for it.

He brushed her cheek with an unexpected kiss as he held the chair out for her. She realized he was staring contentedly at the ring on her finger as she took her seat. She'd had to go back for it when, halfway down the stairs, she'd realized she'd forgotten to put it on, and the look on his face was suddenly well worth the energy.

'My son tells me the two of you have news. I must say, I'm delighted.'

'Well, yes, thank you.' Where was Mark? He'd half convinced her that she wasn't going to make any drastic mistakes, but he should be here to help, shouldn't he?

'What can I——'

'The ring——'

They broke off exactly the same way they'd started, simultaneously. 'Sorry.' She waited politely for him to resume whatever he had been going to say.

'What can I get you for breakfast?' He gestured toward the covered silver serving-dishes lining the gorgeous antique buffet.

When Mark had told her it was a help-yourself-whenever-you're-ready-type meal she had expected cold cereal. 'Please, I can get it,' she protested.

'Fortunately, my problems do not hinder my getting around. Your injury does.' He positioned himself near the food. 'Millie has made a delicious quiche, and there is bacon, ham, sausage. Do you drink coffee?'

She nodded and he passed a cup across the table to her, then filled a plate with 'a bit of everything for a start'.

'Thank you,' she said when he finally rejoined her. 'I didn't expect you to wait on me.'

'My pleasure,' he said. 'Now, what were you going to say before I so rudely interrupted you?'

'I don't see how you could consider this rude.' She indicated the plate. She really wished Mark were here. 'I was just going to thank you for sharing your wife's ring with me.' The ring captured a fractured ray of the bright morning sun pouring through the bay window at the end of the room.

'It's satisfactory, then?'

'More than,' she assured him. 'I can't think of anything I'd rather wear than one that comes complete with a history of happiness. Surely that's good luck.'

'Thank you,' he said, patting her hand. 'If it brings you and my son even a fourth of the joy his mother and I shared, you'll have a very, very happy life together.' He cleared his throat. 'Especially if you love him.'

Her fork clattered to her plate. It was a statement. But the question was in his eyes.

'Do you?' he asked. 'I'm sorry.' He still held her hand and he squeezed it lightly. 'I'm not usually so tactless, but I can't think of a diplomatic way of asking. As happy as I am about all this, I'm afraid I may have precipitated Mark's actions, and I don't want either of you to rush into anything solely for my benefit. I don't have to live your lives if you make a mistake.'

'It has happened awfully fast.' Sarah picked up her fork and rearranged the things on her plate. 'I knew I really, really liked him,' she said slowly. 'More and more every time we've been together, but I hadn't really thought about how much I cared about him because we haven't known each other very long.'

He nodded his head. 'Yes, that's what Mark said.'

She suppressed an inner sigh of relief and warned herself to stick closely to the truth. 'I generally approach things with a little more caution, but when Mark asked me to marry him it seemed so right, and everything seemed to fall perfectly into place.' She met Reggie's gentle stare. 'I've never been in love before but I felt sure that he ... that this was the way it was meant to be ...

It feels like something very special, but I can't tell you I'm sure. Is that love?'

His blue eyes took on a misty glaze.

'Oh, I'm sorry. I know that isn't very reassuring.' She'd blown it. She felt a surge of panic. 'Oh, please, I didn't mean to upset you.' *Where* was Mark?

One corner of Reggie's mouth slowly curved upward. 'Oh, Sarah, please don't apologize. You've just made my day. You sound full of just the right amount of wonder and uncertainty. I can't tell you how much I appreciate your candor.' He stood abruptly, taking both of their cups back to the buffet to refill them. 'I thought I wanted some gushing declaration, but I think it would have left an uneasy suspicion. Suddenly I remember exactly that queasy "am I doing the right thing?" feeling, and I find myself feeling *very* reassured.'

'If it helps, I promise we won't rush into any——'

He turned and the teary-eyed look had been replaced by a teasing twinkle. 'Please, feel free to rush into anything you want.' He sat down beside her again. 'It's obvious Mark told you that the doctors have pre-

dicted I won't be around for long,' he said ruefully.
'I'm not foolish enough to believe that didn't speed
things between you and my son along a bit faster than
they possibly would have happened otherwise. But
that's part of the magic.' He regaled her with the story
of meeting Marcella and marrying her within two
weeks so that she could join him in his first foreign
assignment with the diplomatic corps. 'I saw the same
chemistry between you at the hospital yesterday, and
I'm satisfied with your answer. Very satisfied.'

She felt her face heat and he chuckled. The only
redeeming factor was that she hadn't had to lie to him.

'Now. Since we don't have a lot of time to get to
know each other,' he went on, 'you must tell me
everything you can think of about yourself.'

So she talked, more than was probably wise. She
told him proudly that she was the first member of her
family to graduate from college. She told him about
her family's reluctance for her to accept the
government job in Washington, DC. She had had no
intention of telling him that they all assumed she'd
eventually fall flat on her face and return home, marry
and raise a half a dozen kids, but she told him anyway.

For a moment, he frowned. 'And you don't want
to marry and raise kids?'

'Of course,' she said quickly, realizing what a
blunder she'd made, 'but I also want to do something
myself, make a difference.'

The smile returned to his eyes. 'You're an idealist.'

'I did come here with stars in my eyes and all sorts
of outrageous, unrealistic expectations about what I
could actually do. But I still believe I can help.'

He squeezed her hand. 'If I hadn't believed that, I would never have stayed in the diplomatic service,' he said approvingly.

'And did you make a difference?' she asked.

'I like to think so,' he said. 'If you only look at individual events the world often seems a lot less stable than it was twenty years ago. But on the whole, in far-reaching ways, I think all the governments in the world realize they are accountable for what they do and for their actions' effect on the rest of the world. I think that's a distinct improvement.'

'That's almost exactly what my program was about,' she said enthusiastically. 'Of course on a much smaller scale,' she added, embarrassed.

'What program do you mean?'

She flushed, but warmed to the topic. She told him about the teacher she had worked with during her semester of student teaching, about the study they'd done as one of Sarah's assignments to evaluate a current educational concept. 'We had excellent, excellent results,' she finished weakly, reminding herself that the biggest bores were those who went on too long about themselves and their own interests.

'And that's why you were offered this job working for the Department of Education?' he asked finally, after digging out more details, including that the results of her program had garnered national attention.

'And the whole program was designed to get the students to accept responsibility for their own grades and actions.'

He nodded and seemed almost as pleased as she.

'Do you realize we've been sitting here almost two and a half hours?' she said as he opened his mouth to ask yet another question.

Reggie looked at his watch. 'Goodness! Millie is going to have my head. She won't be pleased to find me exactly where she left me.'

'Where is she, anyway?' Sarah asked.

'Church,' Reggie answered. 'And she ordered me to rest while she was gone.'

Sarah suppressed a grin. He was obviously more worried that Millie would find out that he hadn't followed orders than he was about actually following them.

'Where is Mark?' she asked casually.

'I wondered when you would get around to asking.' He chuckled. 'He and Sam Cortland have been trying for six weeks to get in a game of golf, but something always comes up. They decided to take advantage of the unseasonably warm weather and get it in before winter descends and makes it impossible.'

She wistfully eyed the blur of sun-drenched garden she could see through the frilly opaque curtains. 'It does look nice out.'

'I was a little surprised you didn't go with him.'

'I don't play,' she said. But Mark doesn't know that, she thought irritably. She put her hands on either side of her and pushed away from the table.

'Well, we wouldn't want you in trouble with Millie,' she said, rising. 'You go rest while I clear off the table and take care of the dishes.'

'I can tell you haven't been around here long,' Reggie said, the familiar sparkle appearing in his eyes.

'You invade Millie's kitchen and she'll have your head—right along with mine for letting you.'

She gestured toward the buffet. 'Well, I wouldn't know what to do with all of that, but surely she wouldn't mind if I carry our dirty dishes in?'

'I get the feeling you're determined to find out,' Reggie said. 'Tell you what. You do that if it makes you feel better, and I'll get us a couple of light blankets to ward off the chill. We'll go "rest" and play invalid in the garden together. How does that sound?'

'Fantastic.'

'I'll also get a couple of books from the library. What do you like?'

She didn't imagine for a minute that a bachelor household would be well-stocked with romances. 'Suspense?'

'I just read a terrific one,' he said. 'I'll bring it for you.'

She hobbled out the side door leading from the kitchen a few minutes later. Ignoring offshoots going in various directions and staying close to the house, she followed the little path around a massive rock garden, and soon found the little alcove Reggie had described. It held a suite of white wrought-iron furniture, padded with pastel-striped cushions. She eased herself down on one of the three *chaise-longues*.

Sunlight filled the area which would be shaded by the house later in the day. She closed her eyes and lifted her face to the bright warmth, disregarding the slight nip in the autumn breeze.

Not a murmur of traffic, no sirens that she could hear; she listened to the peace. This was not the Washington, DC she had come to know. If she didn't know better, she would think they were far from the city. Back home even; back in the country.

She heard footsteps. 'You found me, huh?'

A shadow blocked the sun and firm lips covered hers.

Mark. His mouth was cool, yet it warmed her.

His mouth opened slightly, drawing an echoing response. 'That's better.'

She jumped, flattened her hands on his chest. What was she doing? She was putty. All he had to do was touch her and she lost her sanity. She gently tried to push him away. He strained against her hands, dipping his head to plant a kiss just below her ear. 'Dad,' he whispered.

That explained his greeting. But not her instantaneous reaction to it. She exhaled a long breath that came out sounding like a contented sigh, and played along.

'Of course I found you,' he agreed, more loudly. His clean scent enveloped her a moment before his arms did. 'Scoot over, Sleeping Beauty.' He pushed her skirt against her so that he could join her on the long chair.

'Mmm...' He drew her further into his arms, crushing her breasts against the hard wall of his chest. 'Miss me this morning?' he asked.

'Uh-huh. I thought you'd deserted me.'

'But I was grateful for the opportunity to get to know Sarah a little better,' Reggie's voice cut into the conversation.

Mark drew away with a reluctance that would have been very convincing if she hadn't known it was all an act.

'I suppose I'm going to lose her company now.' Reggie settled in the lounger across from them.

'I don't know why,' Mark said, encircling her with his arm. He leaned back, bringing her with him until they were half sitting, half lying on their sides, sharing one chair. It was an unsettling mixture of being held like a baby and snuggling with a lover. 'This looks like a pleasant enough way to spend the day,' Mark added.

'You probably don't need this now,' Reggie remarked, handing her one of the afghans he'd brought. He unfolded the other across him.

'Yes, we do,' Mark said, spreading the coverlet over them both. When his hand slipped back beneath it came to rest on her side, just below the curve of her breast.

Reggie and Mark discussed Mark's golf game, though Mark didn't seem to have any trouble doing two things at once. While he talked his fingers drew patterns on her midriff, then edged beneath the bottom of the loose-fitting knit turtleneck she wore.

It was all she could do not to gasp when his cool hand came in contact with bare skin that suddenly felt unbearably hot. Sarah squirmed slightly, trying to look as if she was getting more comfortable. She cast Reggie a dubious glance, and was relieved to see that he seemed oblivious to what was going on.

Mark's arm tightened under her, settling her even closer against him as the hand inside her top crept higher, surely no more than a quarter of an inch from the underside of her breast. She went totally still, except for the parts of her that were suddenly beyond her control. A fluttering started low in her stomach.

Her nipples tingled, as if in anticipation of his hand moving just a bit further. His voice adopted a pleased tone as he finished whatever he was saying.

'And have you met Sam yet?' Reggie asked her, attempting to draw her into the conversation.

'We've stayed pretty much to ourselves,' Mark answered, sparing her the need. 'Although I met a couple of Sarah's friends when I picked her up from work once.'

'I don't blame you for not wanting to share your time together, but you're both going to have to get out and about sooner or later. It might as well be sooner, so I've decided I can help you out there. Get all the meeting and greeting over at once.' He looked at them as if they should be as pleased as if he'd just announced that he was giving them a million dollars. 'As soon as Millie and I can get one together, I'm going to throw an engagement party for you.'

'How dare you?' Sarah plopped down beside him in his car a little later that afternoon. Her eyes were snapping. She was furious.

Mark released the clutch and sped down the drive. 'What's wrong?' He shifted, glancing her way. 'I thought things were going rather well.' His nonchalance seemed to fuel her anger and he almost expected smoke to spew from her ears.

'What's wrong?' she said, her voice lifting. '*What's wrong?*'

He had to suppress a grin. Having Sarah around was definitely going to liven things up.

'You . . . you . . .'

He came to a stop at the entrance gate, put the car in neutral, and rotated in his seat. They were out of sight of the house now, and besides, he wanted to watch her expressive face. It might prove very interesting. He caught his breath as he rested his arm on the top of the steering-wheel and gazed at her. She was infinitely appealing when she was angry.

'You're not sounding very lover-like,' he admonished teasingly.

'We don't have an audience. I don't have to sound as if I even *like* you.'

He felt his eyes brighten, but somehow managed to bury his amusement under a coating of concern. 'So why don't you tell me what I supposedly have done?'

'The list may stretch to infinity by the time the day is through,' she said.

She seemed small, delicate. She shrank down in the seat and stared at the hands she had clasped in her lap.

'You're mad about the blanket?' He cursed the hint of humor in his voice.

' "Mad" doesn't begin to describe the way I feel,' she said, clenching her teeth. 'And if that were all, it wouldn't be quite so bad.'

Uh-oh, he thought. 'Okay, what else?'

'You just deserted me,' she accused.

'And nothing bad happened, did it?'

She lifted one shoulder in a gesture that was becoming very familiar. 'Depends on what you consider bad.'

'Dad said you and he had a very nice morning.' For a moment, he sobered. 'I don't know what you said to him, but whatever it was he's convinced now that we'll be okay. And, if it's any comfort, he thinks you're right up there with Thomas Jefferson.'

Sarah glanced up at him in surprise.

'That's about as high as you can get in his eyes,' Mark explained. 'For one thing Mom was a distant descendant, and Jefferson is Dad's ultimate idol.'

'It could have been disastrous,' she muttered. 'You lucked out.' She shot him a look of unbridled irritation.

He reached across the short gap between them for her hands, then thought better of touching her. Not at this point anyway. He braced his palm on the stick-shift. 'Do you think I would have gone golfing if I'd thought for a second that you wouldn't be able to handle it? That you and Dad wouldn't hit it off?'

'How should I know *what* you would do?' she said with a heavy layer of sarcasm. 'Do you think I would even be here if I had known this was going to be a one-woman operation?' She looked at him and firmed her lips into a grim line. 'And you used your dad as an excuse to play touchie-feelie.'

This time he couldn't help himself. He laughed.

Her fury, which up to now had obviously only been simmering, came to a full boil. Her hand fisted and swung toward his heart. He caught it, and her hand went limp in his.

'I'm sorry.' Her face paled with horror. 'I don't usually hit people.'

Her dismay wrung his heart and his laugh softened to a gentle chuckle. 'And I'm sorry, Sarah. I don't usually become engaged and then desert the person I'm engaged to.'

His attempt to make her smile failed miserably. 'I should have told you what was going on, given you some idea of what I had in mind.' He lifted the hand he still held and pressed a kiss on her knuckles. 'I'm sorry.'

Something about her went straight to his heart as she primly removed her hand from his and folded them back in her lap. His heart thudded heavily and his pulse felt so strong that he almost expected his veins to break through his skin. The little two-seater sports car he dearly loved was suddenly too small, too hot. He turned back in his seat and rolled his window down halfway. He leaned against the door and let the cool breeze wash over him.

'Sarah, when Sam called me this morning I told him I couldn't play, but I realized leaving you and Dad alone would be a prime opportunity for you to get to know each other.'

'You should have told——'

'I came to your room. You were still asleep.' He paused, remembering the way she had looked, hugging the pillow, entwined in the covers, her hair scattered like unraveled silken strands of rope. Just thinking about the scene made his body react exactly the way it had then. He moved uncomfortably. 'I didn't have the heart to wake you.'

'You could have left me a note.'

I didn't dare come back in that room or I would have crawled right into that bed beside you. 'I could have. I didn't think about it.'

Her next words confirmed his certainty that crawling into her bed would have been a huge mistake.

'That doesn't excuse your pre-pubescent groping in the garden.'

He felt his jaw drop at her choice of words. He wanted to laugh but the warning glint in her eyes stopped him. 'Sarah, that was for Dad. Same as the kiss,' he explained, and earned a look of censure.

'He didn't even know.'

'He knew.'

'How could he?'

'He knew, Sarah. Belive me. Maybe he didn't know exactly where my hands were, but he knows me well enough to know they weren't hanging loosely at my sides.'

'You should have let him think whatever he wanted and kept your hands hanging loosely at your sides,' she said. 'And we'd better set some ground rules. Honestly, you're as bad as Len.'

Len?

'My boss?' she reminded him, answering his unspoken question.

'Your boss at the Pancake Palace?'

'No, the man in the moon.'

The boss he'd wanted to punch yesterday? He *still* wanted to punch him, he realized. 'What do you mean?'

'Oh, Len always had a good excuse for putting his hands all over us.' Rosy spots of color brightened Sarah's high cheekbones. 'He would come up beside me and "check my orders". And, of course, he had to put his arm around my shoulder and let his hand kind of wander down to my...over my shoulder when he did.' She cleared her throat. 'Or he'd stand in the middle of the doorway as I went through so I had to brush against him to get by. Or he'd reach for something just as I passed him and his hand would just happen to graze my hip...'

Mark had never felt so disgusted in his life. No—disgusted didn't come close. His hands wrapped around the bottom of the steering-wheel and his knuckles turned white.

Sarah went on. 'And that was why he was so anxious to attack when that whole accident with your breakfast started.'

Mark felt thoroughly confused. 'What?'

'I had just told him in no uncertain terms to keep his hands off me. He was mad and looking for a way to get back at me when I dropped your breakfast.'

'Why didn't you quit?'

'You mean before or after you quit for me?' Sarah threw up her hands in exasperation. 'I *needed* to pay my light bill. Oh, this is getting us nowhere. I thought we were going to deposit your check and pay my bills.'

He gripped her shoulder and turned her to face him. 'Sarah, sue him.' He could think of better things to do with the boss from hell, but he was fairly sure she wouldn't agree to let him do any of them. 'Let me sue the bas——'

'And you too?' she asked innocently.

He felt himself go white. He released her shoulders. 'But this isn't ... wasn't the same ...'

Her eyes were wide as they locked with his. They squashed him as badly as if she had run over him with a steamroller. She was right. He was as guilty of sexual harassment as Len had ever been. He'd hired her to do a job, then lost sight of the fact. The realization stunned and shamed him.

'Oh, I know,' she continued ever so softly, 'this is different; I know there has to be a certain amount of... of interaction between us if we're going to convince Reggie that we're in love, but——'

'I won't hold you to our agreement if you want out,' he said quietly, forcing himself to meet her eyes.

She suddenly looked confused and uncertain.

'Don't worry,' he added, 'you can keep the check whatever you decide.' He held his breath, terrified of what she'd say.

'What about your dad? We can't let him down.'

He could barely contain his relief at her words. 'Are you sure? You want to go through with this?'

She nodded after a long moment. Again his hands reached for her, but he stopped himself. Touching her seemed to be such a natural part of the arrangement. 'You're right. We have to set some boundaries.' He squared his shoulders. '*You* have to set boundaries,' he amended. 'All you have to do is tell me where you draw the line. I won't cross it,' he promised. 'And I won't do anything you can't defend yourself against without ruining everything,' he finished.

For a long moment neither of them spoke.

Then she smiled as she hadn't smiled all day. Suddenly everything seemed right again. 'That's exactly it. You just have to think, to care about how I feel.'

That was easy. He *did* care how she felt. If he hadn't wanted her to ache as badly as he ached, he wouldn't have taken advantage of the situation in the garden. He was also positive that that wasn't what she meant.

'I do care how you feel, Sarah,' he said.

'Good. Then all you have to remember is not to do anything "undercover" that we couldn't do right out in front of God and everyone,' she said seriously.

He couldn't resist a grin this time. He considered taking her to the mall at the Smithsonian, or to the theater at the shopping center just three blocks down the street.

Sometimes he was amazed at what people didn't mind doing 'right out in front of God and everyone'. She didn't know it, but she'd practically given him license to do whatever he darn well pleased.

Her fingers lightly curved over his forearm. 'Mark?'

Irritation and frustration surged through him. She could touch him but he couldn't do the same? She'd just compared him to the greasy slob in that restaurant and the comparison stung. He jammed the car into gear and roared out past the gates on to the street. 'What?' he growled.

'Can't we talk about just one more thing?'

'Talk. I'm listening.'

'Your dad is getting carried away. An engagement party is too much.'

Oh, no, Sarah. You've won every point so far. Don't expect to win them all. 'Why?'

'If all your friends know, won't it be ten times harder for you after...?' She broke off and revised what she'd been going to say. 'When we break the engagement?'

And *that* was beginning to irritate him. Couldn't she just say 'after your father dies', instead of tiptoeing around it? Why did she painfully calculate every phrase and sentence? 'Frankly, Sarah, you've mistaken me for someone who gives a damn what my friends think,' he said sarcastically. 'I won't have a bit of trouble with it.'

'But——'

He shot her a glance. 'Which bank did you say was yours?'

She named one with a branch near his office building.

She sat stiffly on her side of the car, he sat silently on his, until he had dropped the envelope with her deposit slip and his check in the slot. 'Now where? Who all did you say you owe money to?'

Those big hazel eyes looked like a wounded animal's. Dammit, Mark Barrington, you could have put that differently.

'I need to go to my apartment,' she said quietly.

'For heaven's sake, why?'

'I can't pay everything without the bills and stamps. Then I can take them to work and mail them on my lunch-hour tomorrow,' she said in a rush.

Sh cringed closer to the door every time he moved to change a gear or turn on an indicator. He felt guilty that he intimidated her, but a satisfaction overlaid the guilt. Dammit, he should be shot.

'I'm sure no one will mess with your car,' she offered hopefully. 'Not in broad daylight.'

He loved his car, but it was transportation, replaceable. He knew he should say that, offer his own olive branch, tell her not to worry. Instead he quipped, 'I guess we'll just have to chance it.'

She didn't make any more conciliatory moves. He was glad. He felt like the biggest jerk this side of the Atlantic, but he also felt better by the time they reached her street. Not good enough to apologize, but he felt good enough to offer kindly to carry her up all those wicked stairs once they had parked and were inside the front door of the building.

'That's okay,' she refused. 'I'm getting around much better today.'

'I noticed,' he said. 'I'm glad,' he added.

An honest but skeptical light came back on in her eyes. 'Let's get it over with.'

He watched her slender figure determinedly attack the first flight of stairs. She had the nicest rear end he'd seen in a decade. She'd changed into some type of body-hugging knit pants before they'd left the house and her little wiggle was enough to steal his anger and every last bit of his concentration.

Regardless of what she thought, Reggie had come up with a winner of an idea with the engagement party. The more people that knew about it, the more reason he'd have to show his 'affection' in public.

He inhaled deeply. And for her sake—and his—they'd better stay in public. He didn't know how long he'd be able to keep his promise—or his hands to himself—otherwise.

'Oh, my God.'

He'd been watching her unconsciously seductive moves so intently that he almost ran into her when she stopped.

'What?'

'My apartment,' she whispered as he joined her on the step below her landing. 'I think I've been robbed.'

CHAPTER SIX

THE wooden door was shattered. What was left of it hung at an angle on one hinge.

Mark stepped around her. 'Stay here,' he ordered, then walked slowly, carefully toward the opening.

'Mark, maybe we should call the police,' she whispered near his ear.

He jumped almost a foot. 'I told you to stay back.' He gave her a stern look but at least the mocking, sarcastic tone was gone.

'But shouldn't we call the police?' she hissed desperately.

He stood just inside the door for a long moment. 'Whoever did this is gone.' He held out an arm and she hurried under it. His hand settled on her shoulder and squeezed reassuringly, pulling her closer to his side. 'Somebody did a heck of a lot of damage.'

It was a good thing she didn't have much, she decided, because the little she owned had been sliced, diced and scattered from one end of the room to the other.

The one lonely piece of furniture in the main room, the flowered couch, bore gaping holes that revealed springs and, in places, the wooden frame. What had been cushions were now long, narrow strips of fabric. The stuffing was everywhere. The room looked as if there had been a cotton-ball snowstorm inside.

There were bits and pieces of other things around the room. She actually recognized what was left of two of her favorite blouses. A bra with both cups missing hung like tinsel from the nondescript light fixture in the middle of the ceiling. What some of the items were was anybody's guess. She suspected that the rest of the apartment would look exactly the same.

'Come on,' Mark said, taking her hand, walking her down the hall, 'we may as well see it all.'

She was pleasantly surprised to find a few items of clothing still on hangers in the small closet. 'They missed something,' she said with a forced brightness. She withdrew her best suit.

'Look again,' Mark suggested drily.

'Oh.' An obscene message had been spray-painted in blue letters from top to bottom. 'Why did they have to do that?' She didn't bother taking any of the other things from the bar. She slumped down on the edge of the box springs—the only thing left of her bed. 'They must have wanted the mattress,' she said, looking dazedly about, then she giggled.

Mark eyed her strangely.

'Don't you think it's good that they found at least one of my things worth taking instead of destroying?'

Her explanation brought a chuckle. He eased his considerable length down beside her and folded one of her hands in between the two of his.

'Look at the bright side,' he said. 'If you had a lot of great stuff, this would be a real tragedy. You'd be really upset.'

'Thanks.'

'No problem, ma'am.' He tipped a fake hat. 'Glad to be of service.'

'Why me?' she wailed softly.

He folded her into his arms, pulling her close as a lonely tear escaped from the corner of her eye. 'Just lucky, I guess,' he said. One long finger tenderly wiped the moisture from her cheek. 'I forgot to ask,' he said, holding her away for a second. 'Do you mind if I hold you for a few minutes?'

She laughed and nestled against him again. 'I don't know what I'd do if you weren't here.'

'You probably wouldn't have a problem, then.' His chest rumbled under her ear. 'This is your payback for calling the police about the car.'

She hated to move but reluctantly did. 'So what do we do next?'

'Get some boxes.' He looked around. 'We'll salvage what we can and get you out of here, once and for all.'

'Shouldn't we call the police?'

'Probably. But unless you need to for your insurance——'

'I don't have any,' she said.

'And after the trouble I had just finding a working phone to call them last night...' He let her finish the thought for herself. 'Let's let the manager handle it. And I sincerely doubt they'll be able to do much besides take statements and fill out reports again.'

She agreed. The total destruction nauseated her. She felt violated. Right now, she wanted nothing more than to get out. For good.

By the time they got boxes and sorted through the debris, they had been there three hours.

Among the few things the intruders hadn't messed with were her bills. 'Figures,' she told Mark as they finished. 'They destroyed my yearbooks and photo albums——' her voice caught again just thinking about it '—but they didn't touch these.' She stuffed the bills in her purse.

Leaving the apartment felt like closing the door on her entire past. In two days Mark had come to represent the future.

He carried the big box—her past. She focussed on his broad, strong back—her temporary future. By the time this little 'job' was finished, would she have anything of herself left?

'Damn!' Mark stopped abruptly in front of her.

She peeked around him toward his car, afraid of what she would see.

'They stole my hood ornament,' he said in a flat voice.

'Look at the bright side.' She giggled, offering him back his platitude. 'It would be a "real tragedy" if they'd liked it enough to take the whole car.'

Two evenings later, Sarah returned from work, sagged down on the side of the bed, and slowly started stripping out of the new suit she'd worn to work.

She was in the process of hanging it back in the closet when Mark knocked on the door.

Besides his being the only one in the house who came to her bedroom door, she would recognize his impatient tattoo anywhere.

'Just a minute,' she called, grabbing a long white sweater and forest-green leggings from the drawer.

'Can I come in?' She saw the knob turn, and took her clothes into the bathroom.

'Okay,' she yelled as she closed the door behind her. She wasn't surprised when he knocked on the bathroom door seconds later.

'I'm dressing,' she said, not disguising her exasperation. 'I'll be ready in just a minute.' Not that she expected him to waste precious time.

He didn't. 'You know, I've been thinking...'

Dangerous. After only three days here, she'd learned that those words started many, many conversations in this household. And the conversations they started usually ended with her revealing or promising or saying things she didn't intend to reveal, promise or say in a million years.

'...we should just forget about this expedition for now.'

Yeah. You said the same thing yesterday. 'Did you bring the "For Rent" section from today's paper?' she asked, deciding the best course was to ignore his attempt at reopening what she considered a dead discussion.

'I brought it,' he said glumly. He sounded like a disenfranchised, disgruntled, stubborn little boy.

She brushed a comb through her weather-frizzed hair and wondered why she bothered. The minute she stepped outside in this misty late afternoon it would go wild again, but it prolonged the time when she would have to face him.

'Did you see anything interesting?'

'Not that you can aff——' He broke off, stepping away so that she could open the door wide enough to come out.

'I'm ready,' she said. 'You're not going like that, are you?' He still had on a lawyerly-looking black suit. 'You may as well wear something comfortable.' She cleared her throat. 'Apartment-hunting is going to take some time.'

'That's what I wanted to talk to you about.'

She took the section of this morning's newspaper from his hand and sat down on the side of the bed with it. 'I'll go through here and mark the best possibilities so we can be a little organized about this if you want to go change.'

She grabbed her purse from the end-table and searched for the highlighter pen she always carried.

'Sarah, would you listen to me?'

'You aren't going to convince me not to look for an apartment,' she said flatly, and continued scrabbling through the chaotic mess that seemed to breed and multiply in the bottom of her huge bag. 'I'm not going to change my mind.'

'Would you just look at me?'

Just what I've been trying to avoid. 'No.' But she looked anyway.

He smiled that knowing, wonderful, charming smile. 'Why?' He was propped by the open bathroom door with one hand on the knob and the other fisted at his waist. One foot was planted solidly on the floor while the other was crossed over his ankle and the tip of his highly polished shoe dug a furrow in the plush carpet. His beautifully tailored jacket hung open and his white shirt contrasted vividly with his golden tan. The top two buttons were open at the throat and revealed a few coarse, dark hairs. He was as un-little-boy-like as she'd ever seen and he took her breath away.

'Because you're going to try to talk me into something crazy again.'

'Then don't agree to it,' he said, as if he really expected her to believe that she had a choice. 'Just hear me out. I've been thinking——'

'If you don't want to take me I'll take the Metro, Mark,' she said. 'That would probably be better anyway. I get the strangest feeling you aren't going to be much help.'

His eyes grew a shade darker. His jaw clenched a smidgen tighter. She couldn't tell if he was amused at her or irritated.

'Yesterday, we only talked about whether or not you needed to find another apartment,' he said.

She debated with herself for a minute. 'I already told you, since I was able to catch up my bills with what you gave me, I want to use this paycheck——' she pulled it from her purse—Exhibit A '—to make a deposit on a new place. I don't know what good it would do to rehash the discussion we had last night.'

He slowly walked to where she sat and crouched down in front of her. She watched as he frowned, obviously choosing his words very carefully.

'This is different,' he finally said, 'and I guess we should start with Dad.'

'What about him?' she asked worriedly.

'You heard him last night at dinner.'

'You mean about setting a date for the wedding?' She rolled her eyes.

He nodded grimly.

'That's why I have to get out of here as soon as I can.' She sounded panicky and knew it. She took a deep breath, brought her voice under control. 'You were right about him. I realized exactly why you hurried me out of his hospital room the day you introduced us.'

'You had to fight yourself not to suggest getting a calendar?' he asked.

'I had to bite my tongue not to name a date. Any date. Valentine's Day popped into my head and I had my fork ready to jab myself so I would scream instead of saying it if my mouth so much as twitched as if it was going to open.'

'I'm glad you didn't have to hurt yourself,' he said with amusement.

'How does he do that anyway?' she asked desperately.

'He asks leading questions until you arrive at the answer he wants. Then you're supposed to think the whole thing was your idea in the first place and fall right in line.'

'Wouldn't you say that makes it all the more important that I move out as soon as possible? Before he traps me into saying something we'll both regret?'

Mark absently took her hand and laced her fingers between his. 'That's what I've been thinking about. How do you think I feel? It was all I could do not to tell him we'd get married next week—which is what he was trying to get you to say. He must be losing his touch if you were going to suggest Valentine's Day. You have no idea how difficult it can be also to have the emotional need to please him.'

'You think I'm doing this for my health?' She felt insulted. She reclaimed possession of her hand.

'I thought you were doing it for you. For the money,' he said thoughtfully.

'Well, I am,' she had to admit, 'but that's only part of it.'

'Stop me if I'm wrong, but I don't think you had much choice.' His long legs stretched straight out in front of him and he fixed his attention on the toes of his shoes.

'Of course I had a choice. And if I didn't believe this was the right thing to do, all the money in the world wouldn't have convinced me,' she said indignantly. 'Believe me, I care about your father. If I didn't . . .'

He held up his hands. 'I know, and I'm sorry, but we're getting off track here.' He glanced sideways at her, as if weighing her reaction in advance. 'I think you should forget moving out; we should forget the engagement party next weekend.' He paused. 'We should make it a wedding instead.'

She opened her mouth but no words came.

'The only thing that's going to make Dad content is a wedding, but I'm sure you've figured that out.' He waited for her acknowledgement.

'But——'

'Let's just do it. Otherwise we'll use up the last five months or so of his life fighting him and trying to stay one step ahead of his machinations.'

She started to speak again but he pressed a finger to her lips. Her lips tingled even after he lifted his hand. His blue eyes kept her spellbound. 'You said you care about him?'

She hesitated, certain that an honest answer wasn't in her best interest, but she couldn't help herself. 'You know I do. A lot.'

'And he likes you.' He stood abruptly and started to pace. 'And his death-wish has changed from seeing me happily married to seeing me happily married to you. I don't think we're going to be able to placate him for the rest of his life. He's not easily fooled. I could see the wheels turning last night when both of us just sat there and tried to avoid any comment that would indicate a tentative season at the very least,' he said drily.

'But I told him we didn't want to rush. That we needed more time to get to know——'

'Dad isn't going to give up. A wedding would give him complete peace.'

Her eyes flew wide open. 'He...we were talking about setting a date.' He stopped in front of her again. 'You're talking about actually getting mar——'

This time his lips pressed against her mouth. The palm she raised to push him away rested, then flattened, on his chest. Just as her backbone began to lose its strength he pulled a fraction of an inch away. 'You said you'd hear me out.'

His warm breath teased her lips warningly, and she felt a primal urge to rattle off anything just so that he'd kiss her again to keep her quiet. But common sense took over, and she nodded in agreement.

'We could have a wedding next weekend instead of the party.' He glanced toward the open closet. 'That dress would do just as well for a small, informal wedding as it would for an engagement party.'

Her head turned toward the dress. He'd given her an advance on next month's salary when he'd taken her shopping on Monday night to replace the things that had been destroyed. Then she'd seen this dress and he'd bought it for her because she 'needed it' as part of her job. For the engagement party.

It was the most elegant, extravagant thing she'd ever owned, but it didn't begin to match the dreams of the wedding dress she wanted someday.

But he was right. It would do, she realized. Tiny sequins and diamanté lined the scooped neck and then swirled to suggest a lily or some other simple floral emblem. Its stem narrowed to a point at the softly gathered waist. The salesclerk who'd helped her try it on had described the pale pale pink color as 'blushing white'.

'You're not just talking about setting a date?' she asked incredulously, wanting to make sure that they both understood the same thing. 'You're suggesting a pretend marriage to match our pretend engagement?'

'Yes.'

'Really getting married?'

He nodded. 'The best thing—at least from your point of view, because you could move in here permanently, rent-free. And in the next few months you'd have time to get on your feet, pay off your college loans, put aside something for emergencies.'

'You would still pay me?' she asked, realizing he might be suggesting that her living expenses would take the place of the agreed-upon monthly 'salary'.

'Of course. And no one would think a thing about my wife living with me.' Mark grinned as he used the argument she'd thrown at him yesterday against her. 'They'd think it rather odd if you didn't.'

'You don't think Millie and your dad would think it strange if I stayed in one room and you in another?'

Mark's hand cupped her face; his sparkling dark eyes looked deeply into hers. 'Let's worry about one detail at a time,' he said. 'I think I have that figured out.'

'And what will be next? A pretend pregnancy?'

Sarah pushed him away, pushed past him and marched to the other side of the room. Getting away from him was like emerging from a fog. She was seriously considering his absurd proposal. Had he hypnotized her? She shook her head to clear it.

He swiveled on his heel and eased himself up and on to the edge of her bed. 'That would definitely make Dad happy,' he said wryly. 'But just believing the possibility existed would keep Dad ecstatic for as long as ... for the rest of his life.'

He lunged off the bed and stalked toward her with a predatory grace that made her feel like dinner for some wild animal. 'And Dad and I have to pay our living expenses for this huge house whether you live here or not.' Mark broke into her silence. 'Think how much better off you'll be six or seven months from now.'

Financially—definitely; mentally, physically, in her soul ...? What he was suggesting could be disastrous when they went their separate ways six or seven months from now, after his father died.

Reggie! The thought of that parting already sent a suffocating lump to her throat. She'd already let herself care too much. If she added in her confusing feelings for Mark she could barely think about the future.

'If we continue as we are, I'm still miles ahead of where I was a week ago,' she said. 'And Reggie's happy.'

'Yes,' he agreed, one hand hovering and finally settling over her shoulder as he stopped beside her. 'But at some point, especially if he lives the maximum eight months Dr Hartlie has given him—please, God—he's going to insist on our setting a date. Then he's going to want to be at the wedding. How are we going to put him off that long?'

One of his hands slowly and gently explored the length of her arm. His fingers closed around hers and laced them together when he reached the end.

'We can tell him I've always wanted to be a June bride.' She knew it was weak the minute she said it, and Mark's raised brow told her he agreed.

'Well, that would give him something to struggle to stay alive for,' he agreed, 'but that's only eight months away and, I guarantee you, Dad will make sure we plan and hold a wedding on that date if he's still around.' He tugged lightly and she found herself turning into him. His arm circled her waist and, just by flexing his muscle, he drew her to him. 'He'll be there in his hospital bed if he has to be.'

And how would she ever say she was holding out for a June wedding to a dying man anyway? She could never be that heartless.

'Could I think about this a little while?'

The V in his shirt left by the two open buttons drew her gaze, and her hands crept to his waist beneath his jacket.

'You can have all the time you need. But if we're going to do this instead of the engagement party next weekend, you probably shouldn't take too long.'

'Maybe we shouldn't do it so soon.'

'I wanted to save you the expense and hassle of finding an apartment, moving out... And I thought it might be the easiest way to get out of having the huge, elaborate wedding Dad will want to orchestrate, but if you'd rather——'

'No. I guess you're right.' She frowned thoughtfully. 'The last thing I want is a big wedding. And at least this way we wouldn't have to come up with excuses not to invite my family and make a big deal of it.'

He looked smug and she realized that she'd all but agreed.

'Okay.' She put her acquiescence into words. The light behind his smile was enough to make her want to rethink her decision. 'But.' She held up a finger. 'We have to have some sort of legal agreement. You don't really know me. You should consider that if we make this legal. I could decide I like your lifestyle. I could decide to take you for everything you're worth.'

He sobered and took her face between both his hands. 'Dad's happiness means more to me than anything in my life—ever. I promise you, Sarah J. Fields, you can have anything you want from me.'

She drew away from him and fumbled with the pen on top of the dresser, trying to think of something flippant to say. She must stop feeling everything he said and did so deeply. 'I still think we'd better have the whole thing in writing, just so we remember. Shouldn't be too tough for a legal type like you.'

'If you insist, I'll draw up something tomorrow,' he said. 'But I trust you, Sarah. I don't need——'

'I do,' she interrupted, then added in almost a whisper, 'because I'm not sure I'll be able to keep my emotions out of it.' She told him honestly, 'I always want to know exactly where I stand.'

'But that's the beauty of the whole idea,' he said. 'We can take things as they come. We wouldn't have to end it when Dad...when Dad dies if we didn't want to. Who knows what might happen between now and then? Let's see where this leads us.'

She felt insulated from reality, wrapped in a haze where only he and she existed. Nothing else seemed real except him. Not the room. Not the situation. Not the dress, which she could see from the corner of her eye. He was solid and tantalizing through the thin fabric of his shirt. She deftly withdrew her fingertips from where they'd come to rest on his chest.

'Why should a fake engagement stunt the development of our relationship?' he asked.

Sarah dragged her gaze from his. She wanted to ask if he meant that his feelings, his emotions, were involved now. Or was everything on his part physical attraction? 'So you're suggesting we go ahead and get married in every sense of the word? Like a normal marriage?'

'I'm suggesting we get married and let nature take its course.'

His words were like ice on her bones. The first time she'd listened to that argument, she'd regretted it. She'd decided then that the reason God had given man an analytical brain was exactly to prevent nature always taking its course.

'Now, since we don't have to go look for an apartment for you——' he held out a hand '—let's go tell Dad.'

She started to put her hand in his, and hesitated. 'We're piling up more and more lies and pretty soon they'll all come tumbling down around us. I don't know that I can face him and keep a straight face while you tell him.'

'We were telling lies. With this decision, we aren't anymore. Aren't we doing everything the word engagement implies?'

She had to give him that. She nodded.

'We won't even be making promises we won't keep when we take our vows,' he added.

Her scowl questioned his logic.

'Till death us do part? Isn't that what the wedding vows say?'

It sounded like a prison sentence. 'Yes,' she whispered. But what about the other vows? she wanted to ask. The ones that said love, honor, cherish, and a bunch of other words that should mean something when she said them. She bit her tongue.

'Till death us do part'. Part. Parting. 'Parting is such sweet sorrow'. *Part* was the word she was going to concentrate on, or a year from now she was going to be in terribly bad shape. And all the money in the world wouldn't fix that kind of sorrow.

CHAPTER SEVEN

REGGIE'S wedding present to Sarah was bringing her mother and father to Washington, DC for the ceremony. Had she known, she would have stopped it—*tried* to stop it, she amended.

Having watched Reggie turn a 'simple little ceremony' into a wedding that exceeded her wildest dreams or expectations, she wasn't sure anymore that you *could* stop someone with more money than they could possibly spend in several lifetimes.

But she hadn't planned to tell her parents at all, at least not until it was all over and she could treat the whole experience like just another completed job.

Millie had just gone to get her bouquet from the refrigerator in the kitchen when someone knocked.

'Come in,' she called.

As the door opened she could hear people arriving, chairs scooting across the floor on the lower level. The organist was playing soft, romantic prelude music: 'O Promise Me'.

'We don't have much time,' her father said nervously. He wasn't taking this whole new experience in his stride with nearly as much ease as her mother.

The music swelled through the widening gap in the door as he peeked back out over the activity going on below them. 'Reggie just escorted your mother to her seat.'

Sarah swallowed a gulp.

'I still don't understand why this has to be such a rush-rush affair,' he said as she hurried back toward the bathroom to recheck her reflection in the mirror. 'You're not pregnant, are you?' He asked the question she'd been waiting for since Ben and Mary had arrived early this morning.

'No,' she whispered. 'Reggie—Mark's father—is very, very sick——'

'Looks healthy enough to me,' her dad interrupted.

'He has cancer,' she explained. 'His worst times for now are when he has the chemotherapy treatments.'

She heard the bedroom door open and close again as she examined her face and hair again.

'Come on, Sarah.' Her father peeked into the bathroom. 'It's time.' He held out the bouquet Millie must have brought. 'You look very beautiful,' he said as she stepped out.

His rough tone, the pride in his eyes made her feel like flinging herself into his arms and sobbing. She was suddenly terrified.

Through the open door she heard the majestic strains of the Bridal March. She closed her eyes, took a deep breath. Her mouth was too dry to say anything. A lump the size of Wichita blocked her throat.

'They're all standing up,' he urged, holding out his arm.

She straightened a seam on her dress and rearranged the ribbons on the cascade of red roses flowing over the white Bible Mark's mother had carried when she and Reggie had taken their vows.

'Now, come on.' He tugged her gently toward the door. 'We can't keep all your fancy new friends waiting.' The words were filled with the same disbelief she'd been feeling since she'd first met Mark. She fought the urge to pinch herself to wake up from the dream. Or was it a nightmare? She wasn't sure anymore.

She let her father lead her across the balcony to the top of the stairs.

Concentrate on the details, a small voice inside her whispered as she fought the desire to run in the other direction. She felt her father's overworked muscles bunch under the sleeve of his cheap but new suit.

Her dress was fitted only through the ornate, long-waisted bodice. The skirt was gently gathered and at least she didn't have to worry about tripping on it, she thought. The hemline stopped at mid-calf in front, then swooped almost to the floor in back and swished softly against the stairs behind her, creating a train of sorts.

She kept her gaze on the trail of red roses and huge white bows weaving in and out of the elegantly carved wooden banister to avoid seeing the crush of people, the sea of uplifted faces below.

She could feel their eyes taking her apart piece by piece, examining her clothes, checking out her hair, but couldn't see their raised eyebrows. Then, halfway down the stairs, she felt Mark's gaze.

She looked over the entryway into the den, past the satin-covered chairs filled mostly with strangers.

He looked rich and cultured and powerful in his black tuxedo. His dark hair was groomed as carefully as a small boy's whose mother had dressed him for Sunday school. Mark smiled reassuringly. Admiration gleamed from his eyes. Then his expression turned serious, looking for all the world as if this were

real. It's a façade, she thought. An elegant, mesmer-
izing fantasy, and she would do well not to get caught
up in believing their own drama.

Her grip tightened on her father's arm. He glanced
at her and she numbly forced herself to move on.

Her father's gentle kiss on her cheek as he passed
her to Mark was the next thing that impinged on her
consciousness. The rest of the ceremony passed in a
bizarre blur, as if her mind stepped aside and watched
as her body went through all the right motions. When
the time came her lips woodenly repeated the right
words. '. . . for richer for poorer, in sickness and in
health, to love, cherish, and to obey, till death us do
part.'

Mark's hand tightened over hers and she felt the
clasp in her heart. She squeezed his hand tighter.

'And now I pronounce you husband and wife,' the
minister finally intoned with great enthusiasm. 'Now,
Mark, you may kiss your lovely bride.'

Mark's lips warmed her, banishing the cold
numbness she felt inside. In its place an ache grew,
and she gazed up into his face as he drew away. Tiny,
usually invisible lines networked around his dark eyes
and a pale line surrounded his expressive mouth,
duplicating her tension. Suddenly, her own felt halved.

Then he smiled, and together they faced their well-
wishers.

His father reached for her as the recessional began,
and unashamed tears flowed freely down his face.
He'd coordinated every detail of this perfect wedding,
yet didn't seem the least reluctant to interfere with his
own planned progression of events. She realized anew
why she liked him so much.

'Mrs Barrington,' he whispered, choking on the words as he drew her into a warm and hard embrace. 'I never hoped to live to see this day. As delighted as I am to see Mark married, I'm even more thrilled that he chose you.'

He chose me because I happened to be in the wrong place at the right time, she wanted to protest, suddenly, for some inexplicable reason, near to tears.

Then her parents joined them and the seventy or so guests followed suit. The reception line formed in front of the makeshift altar instead of in the entryway as had been planned. And the rest of the afternoon flew.

Mark and Reggie introduced her to a mass of names, many of them familiar from the national daily news.

She'd added a few friends from work to the guest-list, at Reggie's insistence. They hovered, waiting to congratulate her. She quickly corrected her boss when he hinted that she probably wouldn't return to work now that she'd 'married so well'.

'Don't you dare even think about giving my job away,' she said. 'I will be back in ten days.'

'After a honeymoon in Hawaii.' He rolled his eyes skeptically.

'I *will* be back,' she reiterated, grasping at that one concrete reality.

Guests invited for the reception only rocketed the attendance to over three hundred. They stood beneath one of the three huge canopies Reggie had arranged to have erected on the lawn behind the house. They watched Sarah and Mark continue their performance, applauding and laughing as the happy couple fed each other cake. Then everyone toasted their union with champagne.

Beneath another canopy, tables and a buffet were tended by a small army of servers. And finally, as dusk grew close, a small orchestra began to play beneath the third canopy, where a floor for dancing had been laid.

'I don't think anyone can dance until we do. We wouldn't want to hold up progress,' Mark said, excusing them from a small crowd of well-wishers. 'Do you realize we've never danced together?' he whispered, pulling her close.

'Just don't do anything too fancy,' she pleaded. Her satin high heels were pinching her feet, and the ankle the doctor had declared totally healed had been throbbing for the past hour. And the champagne was beginning to have its own affect, she thought lightheadedly as he swept her into his arms.

'I don't know anything very fancy,' he whispered against her neck, sending vibrations down her spine. 'Besides, our audience will love it if we just stand here and sway.' He tipped her head up with one finger under her chin. 'You can look longingly into my eyes. I can steal a little kiss from time to time.' He did, then pulled her even closer. 'And we'll save the fancy maneuvering for getting out of here soon.'

She sighed, partly in whole-hearted agreement with his suggestion, partly in reaction to his body against hers. His arms around her felt immeasurably reassuring.

'Did you know my folks were coming?' she asked, needing to concentrate on something besides him.

'I made most of the arrangements,' he admitted.

'Why didn't you tell me?'

'Then it wouldn't have been a surprise,' he said, tilting his head as he did just before he started on a fact-finding mission.

'It doesn't matter,' she said quickly. 'It was a wonderful surprise.'

'Dad and I hoped you would feel that way.'

'But what did you tell them? I haven't had much of a chance to talk to either of them and, to tell you the truth, I haven't exactly tried. I'm afraid they might guess and I can't decide if I should tell them the whole truth or...'

Other couples had joined them now and Mark circle-stepped her to a quiet edge of the dance-floor.

One of the other dancers called loudly, 'What's the matter, Barrington? Isn't this private enough for you?'

Mark grinned. His shoulders blocked out the crowd and he lowered his head. 'Might as well give them plenty to enjoy.' This time his lips stayed against hers for long, long concentration-disintegrating minutes.

By the time he raised his head hers was light, frozen in the tilt he'd left it in. Her pulse pounded in a million nerve-endings throughout her body. She kept her eyes closed, trying to force her thoughts back to normalcy. If he were a drug, she was sure she'd be addicted by now.

'If you stay like that,' he threatened softly, 'I'm going to kiss you again, and I'll hold you responsible for whatever happens when we're alone.'

Her eyes flew open and she felt a flush rising to her face. She buried her forehead in his shoulder so that he wouldn't see. 'I'm just trying hard to play my part well, to be convincing,' she managed, and he bent his head to catch the words.

'Anything for the cause,' he said lightly, but his eyes were sadly serious when she looked back up at him again.

'Especially since my parents are here.'

'Darn,' he said mockingly. 'This is all for your parents? For a minute there I almost imagined you were really falling love with me.'

'That would be disastrous.' She borrowed his nonchalance.

'I like them, by the way.' His words matched his slow-spreading, wonderful grin. 'Your parents, I mean. And I think you should let them keep their illusions,' he added somberly. 'It can't hurt them any-more than it does Dad.'

'I hope it's not bad luck that we like our in-laws,' she commented. 'You aren't supposed to, are you?'

'I don't see how that could be anything but good luck. It feels as if we have a head-start.' He stilled for a moment. 'If this were——'

Real. If this were real, she finished for him as he gently began to sway her again.

She strained to see over his shoulder to where she'd last seen her mother and father. Mark turned her, nodding in the appropriate direction.

'I didn't want them here,' she whispered guiltily.

'I know,' he said.

'I feel like two different people, from two different worlds. They're on a collision course and I'm just holding my breath, waiting for the impact.'

'I suspect you worry too much,' he commented.

She shook her head in amazement, staring into his dark, dark eyes. 'You should,' she whispered. 'I might get used to all this and decide I don't want to give it up.'

His voice hardened. 'That's why we signed the agreement, isn't it?' Then his expression softened again and he started to say something else, something she was sure was important. But they were interrupted.

'Hey!' The same voice that had shouted at them earlier called out again. 'Hey, you two! Mr and Mrs Barrington. The music stopped ages ago. Isn't someone else going to get a turn, Mark?'

The entire assembly burst into laughter.

'Not if I can help it, Jason,' Mark called good-naturedly. 'If I wanted to share her, I wouldn't have married her.' The consummate actor, he cocked a disappointed eyebrow in her direction and reluctantly led her off the floor.

Jason, the friend who would have been Mark's best man had it been a traditional church wedding, offered them a toast and the band started up again.

Another toast, another dance. Another toast and Reggie requested 'Chances Are'. 'Marcella's and my song,' he explained as he opened his arms, inviting Sarah to dance. She noted with pleasure that he looked ten times better than he had just a week ago.

Her father's simple toast brought tears to her eyes, then he danced with her.

In time, the sun settled behind the estate walls and the fairy-lights were lit. By the time Mark finally came to claim her again her ears rang and her head spun from the heady combination of compliments, champagne and song. She tried not to look at him with stars in her eyes.

'One more dance,' he said. 'Then we have to go or we'll miss our plane.'

'But Mom 'n' Da——'

'Dad has a two-week agenda planned for them to get through in the three days they're going to stay.'

'We can't leave.' The words tripped off her tongue in a rush.

'Dad will take good care of them. Don't you think people might think it strange if we cancelled our honeymoon?'

'So far away...'

'Dad assures me we'll love his wedding present,' he said drily. 'And you're drunk.'

'I'm not much of a drinker,' she enunciated carefully.

'You should have told me, sweetheart,' he said very tenderly. At least, the words seemed tender as they cut through her haze.

'I did'n' wanna be rude to your friens.'

'They wouldn't have thought a thing. And I could have had the waiter keep you supplied with the non-alcoholic version.' His amused smile filled his voice and made her feel even spacier.

'Ya know how to do everthin',' she said wistfully.

Her mother came to take her upstairs and Sarah faltered slightly. 'You are drunk, Sarah Joy Fields!' Mary exclaimed.

'Barrington,' Mark corrected, supporting her. 'Sarah Joy Barrington. The J stands for Joy, huh?'

Sarah nodded dazedly.

'It fits you perfectly.' He swung her up into his arms, to the applause of the guests remaining.

'It's a good thing we have a long flight,' he whispered as he carried her up the stairs. 'Otherwise, Sarah Joy, I'd be tempted to take advantage of you in your drunken state.'

Conversation passed in a blur as her mother helped her dress in the comfortable knit pant set she'd chosen for their midnight flight. The last-minute rituals—the bouquet, Mark throwing the garter—barely registered.

Then they fled through a shower of rose-petals to the rented limousine Reggie had arranged. As the driver headed for the airport she looked up into her husband's brilliant blue eyes. 'It is a goo...thin'...we have a long fli...' she said thickly.

He pressed her spinning head to his chest. 'Why?' he asked softly. The words rumbled in her ear and she felt his smile.

'I would be tem...ped to *le*' you take avannage of me,' she whispered, then gave in to the urge to sleep before she could make an even bigger fool of herself.

Hell. He'd died and gone to hell, Mark decided as the flight went on endlessly. And he suddenly resented—hated—being married. No wonder he'd resisted taking the plunge till now.

For the umpteenth time he gently pushed Sarah away, back against her own wide, first-class seat, and cursed under his breath as she rebounded like a boomerang. With a sigh and a feminine little snore she recurled herself into him, and snuggled closer to his chest.

'Hell,' he said under his breath.

'I'm sorry?' A pretty flight attendant was passing by and leaned over his seat. 'Can I get you something, sir?'

He saw her gaze flicker over the sleeping Sarah and then light on his newly acquired wedding-band. Sir! If I weren't married, she wouldn't be calling me sir. And the tone of her voice would be different. 'Nothing, I'm just talking to myself,' he said apologetically.

'No problem.' She smiled, started to say something else, glanced at the ring on Sarah's finger, and moved on.

Was this what it was going to be like, being married to Sarah? She turned him on and set him off as easily as she would set an alarm clock. Then he was supposed to keep his hands off her and live with the frustration of wanting her more than he'd ever wanted any woman in his entire adult life.

The flight attendant bent to give the man across the aisle and up one row a drink. He had a great view of her shapely behind, and realized with a start that he hadn't been the least bit interested in anyone else since he'd met Sarah. And now, even if he *was* interested, he couldn't exactly act on impulse. He was a married man. A married man who'd insanely agreed to forgo the only benefits of the state.

Sarah's limp hand slid several inches higher on his thigh. He groaned and prayed for the flight to end. What he needed now was distance from his new bride. He breathed a little easier when he realized that they wouldn't have to work so hard at keeping up appearances in Hawaii. That would be his salvation.

However, as soon as they arrived at their exclusive and isolated hotel on the Big Island, the entire hotel staff seemed determined to contradict his assumption. The native doorman winked at him as he helped Sarah from the limo his father had arranged to pick them up at the airport. A representative of the hotel—a beautiful young woman in a long floral muu-muu—circled their necks with heavenly-smelling leis, presented with the usual kiss on the cheek. 'The traditional welcome lei,' she explained, pointing to the simpler one. 'And, of course, a wedding lei.' She indicated the second, more extravagant one with a knowing smile.

Then, as they were heading for the elevator, a walking nightmare came toward him, grabbing his hand, pumping it vigorously. 'Mark!' Barry Brody called out excitedly. 'We got the invitation the day we were leaving home. I'm so sorry I missed the wedding. Is this the new bride?' He turned eagerly to Sarah and Mark groaned inwardly.

Only when the bellman suggested that he would go on with their things did Mark manage to extricate them.

Minutes later they were at the door to their room, and the bellman presented them with their key as he welcomed them into the honeymoon suite.

The man had barely carried their suitcases into the bedroom when a huge floral arrangement was delivered from Reggie. That was followed by a basket of fruit, nuts, cheeses and champagne from the hotel. The staff member who had brought it refused the tip Mark offered and showered them with Hawaiian phrases, which Mark was certain were romantic good wishes. Then he complimented Mark on his beautiful *wahine*—wife, he explained to Sarah in an aside—and finally they were alone.

'Whew,' Sarah said. 'Was that all traditional Hawaiian hospitality or is Reggie somehow responsible?'

'A bit of both, I suspect.' Mark looked at her ruefully. 'And I think this is going to be a little more difficult than I anticipated.'

'What do you mean?' she asked, making her way to the sliding glass doors leading out to a balcony. She stared out toward the exotic shoreline as he gathered his thoughts.

'I assumed we would be fairly nameless and faceless once we got here,' he said.

She looked briefly over her shoulder, questioning him with her eyes.

'I really thought that once we arrived we could, for the most part, do our own thing. I planned to play golf; you sounded as if you wanted to explore the island. I think, for the first couple of days anyway, we're going to have to act like honeymooners.'

'You don't honestly believe that word will get back to your father?' she asked stiffly. Something about her tone made him want to see her face, but she wasn't looking at him.

'Would it matter if it did?' he said, as much to himself as to her. 'He wanted us married. We are. But on the other hand, will it hurt us to keep on doing what we're doing?' As soon as he said it, he knew it would. His body was already responding to the situation. They were in a hotel room—the honeymoon suite, dammit. He had to distance himself, stay away from her.

'I'm sorry,' she offered, turning at last to face him.

'What for?' he asked gruffly.

She frowned uncertainly. 'I'm not sure.'

His first impulse was to take her in his arms, soothe the uncertainty away. Instead he excused himself, to take the cold shower he'd promised himself.

'Where are you going to sleep?' she asked as he re-entered the bedroom where she was unpacking a little later.

'One of the couches in the sitting-room turns into a bed,' he assured her. 'I checked.' If it hadn't driven him so crazy he would have been amused by her horror as he flipped back the bedspread on the king-size bed as he spoke. 'But for now I think I'll nap here. I'm exhausted.'

'You didn't sleep at all on the plane?'

'I dozed a couple of times, but never could get to sleep,' he mumbled, lying down, closing his eyes, anxious to block her from his view. He thumped the pillow beside him. 'Feel free to join me,' he said drily.

The last thing he heard was her scurrying out of the room.

The sun was sliding down the bright sky when Mark found Sarah later.

She sat in the sand, a good quarter of a mile from the hotel, her body curved toward the sea, arms draped loosely around her legs, her chin practically on her knees. The gentle breeze teased tiny strands of fly-away hair while the rest curtained her face.

'Sarah?'

She looked up at him. Her somber face broke into a smile. 'Mark. You found my note?'

She moved to get up and he extended a hand. She brushed at the fine sand plastered to her provocative shorts and legs. He started to help, but quickly drew back. Damn. It was foolish to be jealous of sand.

Ten days. How was he ever going to survive ten long days filled with nothing but Sarah?

'Did you have a pleasant afternoon?' he asked, remembering the deck of cards he'd found on the table by the balcony.

'If we're going to fool anyone, you should act as if you *know* whether I did or not.' She smiled sheepishly, then flushed. 'I can't believe you slept away your first afternoon in Hawaii.' She gazed out toward the gently rolling waves.

'I didn't realize we would be so isolated,' she said as they walked slowly back to the hotel.

His fingers accidentally brushed her hip and he linked his hands behind his back. 'Why do you think this particular resort has such a reputation for honeymoons?'

Her mouth formed an understanding 'O'.

'What would you like to do this evening?' he asked.

'Did you have something in mind?' She stooped to examine a shell lying on the beach.

Loaded question. He would answer honestly if he thought he could endure hearing her response. 'I thought we might have a quiet dinner in the hotel restaurant.'

She didn't object.

'I'm still beat.'

She stopped in front of him. Her fingertip absently advanced toward the dark circles he knew were blooming beneath his eyes. 'Maybe drinking all that champagne at the reception wasn't such a bad idea,' she said. 'At least I slept like a baby on the plane.'

He reached for her, then dropped his arms back to his sides.

'This is getting more and more complicated, isn't it? Neither one of us knows how to act.' She shook her head. Her flying hair seemed to cast golden sparks in the afterglow of the sun.

'It doesn't have to be.' He risked the touch this time. His fingers closed around her shoulder. 'Sarah, we started all this as friends. I don't see why a marriage license and a ring should change that.'

'It shouldn't, but somehow it has.'

'I know.' Damn right it has, he thought. For some reason his body had heard all those words about two becoming one and it was ready, willing and addicted to the idea. He bent, picked up a large piece of shell and heaved it as far out to sea as he could throw it.

'Let's just pretend this is any vacation. We just happened to come together. We can do what we want, enjoy each other's company...just keep being friends.' He smiled. She made him smile a lot, come to think of it. He let his hand wander down her arm, savoring the feel of her warm, satiny smooth skin.

'Could we go to the luau tomorrow night?' she asked eagerly.

'Sure,' he said. 'I'll make reservations tonight when we have dinner.' He lifted her hand, straightening his mother's rings on her finger, then released her.

She was ominously still for a long time, then backed a step away. 'I'll go change clothes for dinner.'

'Everyone seems to dress very casually. I'm sure you're okay.'

She looked down at herself, grimacing. 'I'm dirty.' With a toss of her head she added, 'I'll race you back to the room.'

'You don't stand a——'

'On your mark, set, go.' She was off, her slender legs flying.

He caught her as they reached the strip of lawn bordering their wing of the hotel. He wanted to tackle her, throw her to the shadowy splotch of grass between the rocky shore and the building. The power of the surf pounded through his heart and veins, not from exertion, but from the insane need to grab her, haul her to him and kiss her until she couldn't breathe, until she was rendered as senseless as he felt. He didn't dare go in with her.

He blocked the door at the end of their wing. 'I'll meet you for drinks over there.' He waved in the direction of the poolside bar. 'Since I haven't done anything since my shower except sleep, I should be okay.'

She looked up at him expectantly as he reached to open the door.

She's not offering an invitation, he reminded himself, staring at her parted lips. She's just waiting for you to open the door. He kissed her lightly anyway, drawing very reluctantly away as he felt her mouth move in an infinitesimal response. 'For any audience we happen to have,' he murmured, then did his gentlemanly bit.

Her head dipped as she slipped inside, and he stood rooted to the spot until the door finally closed, blocking her completely from view.

Ten days. How was he ever going to survive ten long days of this torture?

CHAPTER EIGHT

MARK was embarrassed by her. They'd been married—and honeymooning—a little over a week, and things between them were becoming more and more strained. Sarah was sure it was his embarrassment. And she couldn't blame him or seem to do much about it.

Now he was looking at her as if she'd suggested they take a suicide dive off one of the island's many high, stark cliffs.

'I tried snorkeling once,' he said quickly, 'and frankly I wasn't impressed.' He studiously avoided looking at her as he handed back the brochure she'd shown him with gear-rental information in it. 'Besides, Barry Brody and I finally arranged that golf game I promised him.'

She tried not to show her disappointment as he occupied himself with folding the small map marked with private places for using the equipment and handed it back to her.

'Listen,' he suggested, 'I've heard several people talk about an organized outing twice a week that includes the rental of the equipment, instruction and a shuttle bus to a popular spot on the other side of the island. Let me make arrangements for you——'

'Thank you. That would be nice,' she said, and turned away.

'Sarah?'

She swung to face him hopefully.

He glanced at his watch. 'I have to go. I'll miss our tee-off time.'

'That wouldn't be fair to Mr Brody,' she said, trying hard not to be sarcastic.

He hurried off to his game as if demons were after him.

They had gone to the luau the second evening. She'd laughed and oohed and ahhed. She'd enjoyed the food, the beautiful customs, the native dancers. It was very romantic, she had thought, until she'd smiled up at him when two of the singers had begun the 'Wedding Song'. He hadn't been smiling at all. He'd been staring at her. That was when she'd looked around and realized that they were surrounded mostly by tourists and that she was acting just like them. After that she'd tried to mimic him, becoming very subdued and sophisticated. She couldn't remember her inebriated state at their reception without hot color flooding her cheeks. That was surely the most humiliating thing she'd done and she was mortified just thinking about his having to endure it while his friends looked on.

Then she'd appalled him again when they'd taken a taxi into Kona another day. They'd strolled the streets and shops. He'd stood by as she'd stroked and admired various souvenirs, then selected inexpensive trinkets, like shell leis and coffee-beans, for her friends and family back home.

He'd reached for some of the more expensive things she'd carefully put back on the shelves and pulled out his wallet and she'd realized that she had humiliated him again.

'I want to do this myself,' she'd said quietly, honestly believing that the mementoes she took to people back home had to be what she could afford, not what he could. But she'd promised herself that she would be very careful not to let his friends and associates see her 'cheap' gifts. And she had let him pick and pay for Reggie's.

She didn't know what to think any longer; she just wanted this to be over. This crazy replica of a honeymoon seemed to be building a solid, insurmountable brick wall between them.

After Mark left Sarah dawdled over breakfast, and was on her way to her room to spend a few hours with her deck of cards, enjoying a rousing game of solitaire, when a woman tentatively touched her arm.

'Ma'am?' the woman asked.

Sarah was instantly concerned when she saw telltale streaks of make-up down the woman's cheeks and her swollen pink eyes.

'I wondered if you might be interested in buying a half-price ticket for a helicopter tour of the island,' the woman said quickly.

'What?' The statement wasn't at all what Sarah had expected.

'You see, I bought this ticket a couple of days ago—the tour is this morning—and now I have an emergency at home. I can't go. I thought—hoped—maybe someone could enjoy it since I can't. And, well, frankly, I would like to recoup at least part of my money.' The woman's flustered expression said much, much more than her words.

'I'll bet you could get a refund,' Sarah suggested.

'If I had time, perhaps,' the woman agreed. 'But the tour leaves in another half-hour and I have to be at the airport to catch my flight in less than twenty minutes. I just don't have time.' She shook her head and checked her watch. The bellman came up behind them, with the woman's bags. 'I just saw you by yourself and thought maybe...'

'How much?' said Sarah impulsively. The woman named a figure that sounded very reasonable, though it would have paid Sarah's utility bill several weeks ago. The realization that her own crisis was really over, that her own financial situation had taken a definite turn for the better, freed some restless craving inside her. And right on the heels of that thought came the one that she didn't have to stay at the hotel just because Mark wasn't with her.

Sarah went directly to the desk and the woman followed, giving her detailed directions for the flight. Ten minutes later, ticket in hand, she climbed on the shuttle that ran to various points around the island with the same sense of independence and adventure that she'd felt when she'd set off for Washington, DC shortly after her graduation.

The exhilaration hadn't dimmed when she returned late that afternoon.

'Jim.' She curled her extended fingers into his deeply tanned hand. 'I can't begin to thank you for giving me such a wonderful day,' she said.

'It doesn't have to be over.' He held the handshake when she would have let go. Jim, the best-looking man she'd seen in a long while next to Mark, was a war hero—a pilot in the Gulf War—turned free-spirited helicopter-tour pilot, who flirted with volcanos and chased the sun. He'd shown her parts of the island that she couldn't have seen any other way. And his attentiveness throughout the day had stroked her ego—something she sorely needed after the last few with Mark.

'And I'm flattered that you want me to have dinner with you, but I can't. Really.'

'Just go check. If your husband isn't around you may as well come with me for a few more hours. Leave him a note. There's so much you haven't seen. I swear, you would ooh and ahh over a damn *manu*.' He winked, adding, 'A bird.'

She couldn't help smiling. He'd been feeding her hunger for Hawaiian names and phrases all day.

'Come to think of it,' he went on,' you *did* ooh and ahh over a bird. Let me show you more.'

Sarah heard a snarl, saw a neatly manicured hand come between her and the pilot. The hand gripped the front of Jim's bright floral tropical shirt. 'My wife isn't going anywhere with you,' Mark growled.

'Mark!'

'Where the hell have you been, Sarah?' He didn't release his hold on Jim, just pushed him aside, an arm's length away, and stopped face to face with Sarah.

'Quit it.' Sarah impatiently stepped between them, physically uncurling Mark's fingers from Jim's shirt. She couldn't imagine Mark actually getting violent, but she wouldn't have attributed this aggressiveness to him either.

His sheepish look confirmed that he hadn't acted typically.

'I went on a helicopter tour of the island,' she offered, and felt her eyes light with excitement all over again. 'Oh, Mark, I saw a live volcano. It was . . .' She struggled to find a word that would describe the experience. 'It was phenomenal.'

'Too bad you couldn't have been there,' Jim said just a shade sarcastically.

'I'm sorry, Mark,' she broke in quickly. 'I should have left you a message, but this came up at the last minute and I didn't think of it. Besides, I thought I'd be back long before you. But then Jim . . .' She pulled him forward. 'Jim was the tour pilot and we had lunch, then he showed me a few other things around the island. Jim, I'd like you to meet my husband.' Describing Mark that way made her tongue feel thick and clumsy. 'Mark Barrington.'

The two men eyed each other warily. 'I've enjoyed every second of showing your lovely lady our beautiful island,' Jim finally said. 'She's an absolute delight.'

'Yes, she is,' Mark said tonelessly.

Sarah shifted from one foot to the other.

'I was just telling her, I'd love to show her more. Both of you are welcome. We could check out Kaimu from the ground—that black sand beach you wanted to see,' he said in an aside to Sarah. 'Then we could kick on over to the other side of the island, take in a little bit of Hilo, have dinner . . .'

Out of the corner of her eye, Sarah saw Mark's fist clench at his side. As innocent as her outing with Jim had been, she knew this weird threesome would never work. 'Jim, thank you, but can we take a raincheck?'

'For which year?' Jim said drily, subtly reminding her that their paths weren't likely to cross again. All day he'd been showing and telling her that nothing in life was predictable, not even the land that was constantly being shaped and reshaped by the goddess Pele.

She shook her head helplessly.

He accepted her decision with the same air of unconcern that she'd envied all day. 'You have my card, Sarah,' he said, then gave a thumbs-up to them both. 'Call me if you're at loose ends again. *Mahope*—later,' he explained, heading for the red Jeep he'd parked at the end of the hotel's circular drive.

Sarah sighed regretfully. It *had* been a wonderful day. She turned back to Mark. For a moment she interpreted the look on his face as jealousy, and her heart caught hopefully in her throat.

'I was getting ready to call the police,' he said grimly. 'I came back at ten this morning looking for you and I've imagined you raped, murdered, kidnapped, swept out to sea...' He raked his fingers through his dark hair with exasperation. 'I thought something disastrous had happened. I was on my way to ask the hotel to call the police so I could report you missing.'

She didn't understand the sinking feeling as she realized his reaction was simply worry. The clog in her throat suddenly tasted bitter. In a similar situation he would have been worried about any friend. His concern didn't mean a thing.

She bit her lip. 'The last thing I wanted to do was worry you.' She gazed down at the cool stone floor of the lobby.

'Oh, Sarah,' he whispered softly. 'I'm sorry. I behaved despicably to your friend when I should have been thanking him for showing you the things I haven't.'

The way he said 'your friend' tore another hole in her heart.

'I'm really sorry too,' she whispered, aware suddenly that the sentiment covered much, much more than it implied. What she wanted from him wasn't simple, friendly, genuine concern.

And, for the first time, she *admitted* to herself that she'd fallen in love with him.

She'd known since they'd arrived. She'd known it when she'd felt such pride when he'd introduced her to Reggie's friend as his wife. She'd known it when, exhausted, he'd insisted on walking with her on the beach. She'd felt protected, cherished.

Then, on the beach, he'd looked at her, the longing to kiss her so apparent that *her* mouth had watered. Then she'd bitten her lip until it bled, and she'd known, but denied what she felt. Because he didn't feel it. He felt a fierce sexual attraction and friendly concern. Nothing more.

'I . . . I didn't mean to worry you.' What else could she say? She could hardly apologize for falling in love with him. 'I think I need a shower,' she said abruptly, pulling her sticky blouse from her back. 'It was really muggy this afternoon.'

Mark followed her around the front desk to the bank of elevators. 'Sarah——' he started as the elevator doors closed them in.

'Did you call your father today?' she interrupted.

He nodded, his lips pursed.

'I'm sorry I wasn't here for that,' she apologized again, staring up at the numbers as they rose. 'I hope it didn't embarrass you or cause any awkwardness when I wasn't here.'

'I told him you were napping. The chemo went much better this time. He's in great spirits and already home, resting. He was in a great mood. Our marriage has done wonders for him.'

'Good,' she said as the elevator stopped at their floor. 'Then I guess this has all been worth it.'

Sarah had her keys out before they got to their suite. Mark took them, opened the door, and let her step past him into the air-conditioned cool of the room.

'Has it, Sarah?' The muscle in his jaw tightened, squaring his chin and sending a ripple up one side of his face before the line hardened and looked like sculpted granite. His intensity sent a nervous tremor through her stomach as he caught her arm. Every nerve-ending in her body centered where his fingers lightly touched her.

His eyes captured hers, then his arms did the same, circling her, drawing her close. 'We go home in three days. Don't you think we need to talk?' he asked.

'I told you I'm sorry, Mark. I don't know what else I can say. I should have left you a message——'

'About us, Sarah. We need to talk about what's going on with us.'

She focussed on the rock-solid bit of chest exposed by the two open buttons of his dark polo shirt, afraid to look up at him. 'I didn't realize *anything* was going on with us.'

'Maybe that's the problem. We came here as friends and now we're treating each other practically like strangers. We're avoiding each other.'

She finally met his eyes. '*I* haven't avoided *you*,' she said painfully.

'You're right,' he agreed, and she flinched at his honesty. 'When we've been in the suite you've stayed in one room playing solitaire and I've stayed in the other. That's been my fault.'

'I shouldn't expect you to keep me company and entertain me,' she said. 'I had unrealistic expectations.'

He groaned and rolled his eyes. I had them too, he thought. Oh, lord, so did I.

'Oh, Sarah,' he said sadly, 'we've played a huge practical joke on the world and ended up fooling ourselves more than anyone else.'

She licked her dry lips. 'I . . . I'm not sure what you mean.' The tingling in her skin where he was touching her had turned to fire. His breath felt soothing on her cheek.

'We have the paper, we have the ring, we have the vows. We even have enthusiastic parental approval. What more could we possibly need to quit playing this silly game of "let's pretend"? Do you have the slightest idea what knowing we're really married does to me? What you do to my sanity?' he asked.

Sarah's heart pounded so loudly that she was sure he would hear it. 'I'm only human,' she whispered, and felt him smile.

'Are you? I've wondered.' His lips began a dedicated foray up her neck, past her jaw, drawing nearer and nearer her mouth. 'You've been so cool.'

Her knees got weaker and weaker. She wondered if he would catch her if they gave way. Then his hand descended down her back, steadying her, tracing her spine, pausing at her narrow waist. He followed the curve of her hip and molded her against him, his body lending her support as he pulled her closer still.

'Oh, Mark,' she whispered as his lips paused a millimeter from hers.

His chest rumbled with a low, deep sound that was almost a growl.

'This is crazy, Mark,' she managed to add.

'Is it?' He closed the very short distance between them with tentative, soft-as-sigh kisses that stirred her very soul.

Her hands automatically groped for a firmer hold, and she braced them against his chest. The earth-shaking heat that engulfed her from the inside out felt as powerful as the fascinating volcano had looked. One hand found and clung to his waist as the other came to rest behind his neck with her fingers laced through his hair. He turned the butterfly touch on her lips into something firm and demanding.

'Surely you've noticed how much I enjoy kissing you,' he murmured.

Her breath caught in her lungs, filling them until she was certain they would burst. Finally, somehow, she found the strength to push herself an arm's length away.

'If you deny you liked that, you're lying,' he said huskily.

There was no way she could deny it. She didn't try. 'Liking it doesn't mean we should let raging hormones totally annihilate our common sense.'

'I outgrew raging hormones about twenty years ago.' His chuckle was soft, deep. 'I remember those years all too well, and if raging hormones were controlling me I'd act first and think later. Right now, I know exactly what I'm doing. What I want to do,' he amended. His fingers tightened, pulling her into him as if to prove the effect she had on him. 'I start anticipating the next time I get to caress you the minute I let you go.' He held a finger to her lips. 'And don't say I haven't been absolutely politically correct since we talked a couple of weeks ago. I haven't been out of line once.'

'You've been a perfect gentleman,' she acknowledged.

'I don't want to be any longer. I want to be your husband. I want us to be in that bedroom. Making love.'

She waited for him to say more. She needed him to say more. Terror of what she might say rendered her speechless.

'If this situation had evolved naturally we would be lovers by now,' he told her with a conviction that was scary.

'If this situation had evolved naturally we wouldn't even *know* each other,' she managed to contradict him, silently applauding her common sense.

'But we do. And I can feel your response to me. Don't you think it's time to carry the charade a step further?' he murmured, allowing her to pull away from him for air.

She felt herself go still. The charade? He'd just admitted that the problem was that it all seemed too real. Yet now he called it a charade? Wasn't anything besides his body involved? Her arms stiffened, but instead of pushing him away, as she intended, her hands molded themselves to the hardness of his chest. She was so confused. Her mind and body battled with each other. 'How can you even think that we should become lovers when you just called this a charade?'

'Bad choice of words,' he muttered. 'That doesn't mean we shouldn't do what comes naturally. Don't you think it's time, Sarah, to make this marriage real?'

Love, Mark. What about love? How can it be real without love? She waited, her eyes closed, for him just to mention one word about feelings. She'd probably settle for 'like' if he would just admit that he felt something. Tears burned the inside of her lids.

'Let's just play it by ear. See what happens,' he suggested.

That gave her the strength to push him away. 'I've seen what happens when you just do what comes naturally,' she croaked. 'I don't want to see it again.'

'What do you mean?'

'The summer before my senior year in high school I got all the education I needed on the subject.' She turned her face away from him.

'Someone hurt you?'

'Oh, yeah. Sean hurt me. But I guess I should be grateful. I learned a lot that summer.'

Mark gently pushed her back into the easy chair and took a seat on the pillowed foot-stool, giving her his undivided attention. 'You want to tell me about it?'

'Not really,' she said, casting him a sideways glance.

He took the fingers of one hand and laced them through his. 'But will you?'

She closed her eyes wearily. 'Sean's father was the president of the local bank. Sean was every girl's dream and that summer, before our senior year, Sean decided he liked me.' She lifted one shoulder helplessly. 'He was totally devoted to me, and late that July and all through August Sean and I were a hot, hot item—in more ways than one,' she added.

Mark started to interrupt.

'I almost gave him my virginity. I certainly gave him my unadulterated devotion, my heart and soul, such as they were.'

'And in return he gave you . . . ?'

She shrugged. 'A few gifts and trinkets. A cassette I'd been wanting. A fairly cheap necklace that was the most expensive piece of jewelry I'd ever owned.'

He took a deep breath and she matched it with one of her own. 'We only had one class together that fall and I had a job in the evenings,' she went on, 'so I didn't really think much about our not seeing each other much once school started. But I assumed we'd go to the first dance together that second week of school.'

'And he didn't ask you?'

She shook her head. 'He not only didn't ask, I totally humiliated myself two nights before the dance—the first time we'd seen each other all week. I told him how anxious I was for him to see the beautiful new outfit I'd bought for the dance.'

'It seems like a logical assumption to me.'

'That's what I thought.' She laughed without humor, but went on determinedly. 'He told me he had to take Jennifer Powers—you know, head cheerleader, her father was on the city council. He said his parents expected it. And that was that.' She brushed her hands together, then folded them primly in her lap, away from his.

'So would you please explain what all that has to do with you and me?' he asked, irritation smothering his voice. 'And I should warn you that if you plan to compare me to Sean I do believe I'll wring your pretty little neck,' he added.

'I was strictly telling you past history. And past history tells me that our backgrounds are too different. Eventually we'll come to the same parting of the ways. When we get there I don't want to have more invested than I'm ready to lose.'

'What aren't you ready to lose?' he asked softly.

'My self-respect.'

He touched a strand of her hair, separating it from the rest then stroking it back into place. 'I don't see why we'd necessarily come to a parting of the ways. Sean obviously never really cared about you.'

'Do you know, to this day I really can't say that? I know it's probably some sort of protective mechanism but I still believe, deep down inside, that he cared for me.' She defended her first love, despite the fact that he'd left a deep and painful scar. 'He just didn't like me enough to deal with our differences. I was an interesting diversion.'

'So what does he have to do with us, Sarah?'

'We don't fit any better than Sean and I did. Can you see us married for the long term?'

'So you want a guarantee?'

'There aren't any guarantees,' she finally said. I want love, she thought, and held her breath. That's enough.

She couldn't stand his silence and broke it. 'When I get married for real—which I'm not in any hurry to do—I don't want it to be a fling. I want to be somewhere where I belong. And I want to at least *try* for forever.'

'And I don't fit into your picture of forever?' he asked.

'I don't think you believe I fit into yours either,' she said. This time she stood, gingerly moved past him and went to the lanai door.

He moved behind her, not touching her, just inches from her shoulder. If he would touch her, maybe——

'Sarah,' he asked softly, 'does it make any difference that you're the only person I've ever asked to marry me, the only woman I've ever even considered marrying?'

'It would if we'd married for the right reasons,' she whispered. 'For love. We went into this as a temporary thing.' She swung to face him. 'You wanted to make your father happy. I needed your money.'

He flinched.

'See? That bothers you. Even if we change the terms of our agreement now—which is a bad idea because the decision would be based on desire—how will you ever deal with that reality? That difference will always be between us.'

'Then will you explain why I don't think about it now—until you point it out? Sarah, I haven't been attracted to anyone else since I met you. I don't see that changing.'

'Enforced familiarity.'

'Sarah——'

'I learned from Sean not to let my hormones override my common sense. My common sense says it would be disastrous if we changed the game-plan now.'

She felt his hard gaze digging into her soul. Then he turned abruptly on his heel and walked out of the room, slamming the door behind him.

She wrapped her arms around her waist. She'd won the battle—both with him and with herself. So why did she feel as if she'd just lost something very important? And why did she feel like crying? With him gone, it didn't matter. So she cried.

CHAPTER NINE

MARK left a note telling her where he was playing golf for the day and a key to a rental car for her on the desk the next morning. For the last three days of the honeymoon they managed to avoid each other.

Now they were on the plane going home. About an hour out of DC, he lifted her hand casually. 'I've been thinking about our talk the other day,' he said.

'What about it?' she asked hoarsely, too tired from the long flight to have her defenses against him firmly in place.

'You're wrong,' he said, spreading her fingers and lacing his with hers. 'You accepted this position as a matter of economics. That doesn't mean that when the position changes you can't change your attitude about it.'

'Maybe you're right,' she said. 'Past experience tells me that you don't mix emotional decisions with financial ones. And I don't mix business with pleasure.'

'But if you can combine the two, can't you have the best of both worlds?'

'Only if the two people sharing the experience are from the same world, so they are combining apples and apples instead of apples and oranges,' she said.

They had their seats leaned back almost as far as they could go. Sarah turned a bit in hers so that she could see him.

'I guess it's time for honesty, Sarah,' he said.

'Probably past time,' she told him.

'Remember when I told you to let me worry about how we would carry this off once we were home from the honeymoon if we were sleeping in different beds?'

She nodded. 'You said you had something in mind.'

He grinned ruefully. 'I did. I assumed we would be sleeping in the same bed by now.'

She didn't know whether to be angry or amused. How could she help but love him when he was such an optimist? He was the missing part of her that she needed because, try as she might, she just couldn't seem to see everything through a rosy tint. She chose the amusement. 'So I guess you'd better think fast,' she said, looking at her watch. 'I'd say you have a little over an hour and a half to come up with something.'

'Or you could give up and just let me sleep in your bed.'

'Maybe we could get a bundling-board like they used to use to separate young couples.'

He groaned, and she thought with a strange sense of contentment that at least they were talking again.

The easy camaraderie lasted until they were home and Reggie was throwing his arms around them. And he was glowing, whether they were or not.

It's all been worth it, Sarah reminded herself as Mark and Millie carried their things to the master suite on the second floor.

'So how was the honeymoon, Sarah?' Reggie asked, drawing her into the garden-room at the back of the house. Sarah was touched by the carefully laid snack tray, complete with a few thawed pieces of wedding cake and fresh pineapple sticks from the case they'd sent ahead.

'Hawaii was wonderful,' she said. 'And I would almost bet you and Marcella had the same rooms Mark and I did.'

'Sixth floor?' he asked.

She nodded.

'I asked if they still had the same one when I called for the reservations and they offered a choice of that or one with better beach access,' he confirmed, raising an eyebrow warily. 'I hope you didn't mind; I chose the one a little further from the beach——'

'We loved the rooms, and the view was spectacular,' she assured him.

Mark came in then, and changed the subject to his father's progress. 'How did your treatments go last week?' he asked.

Reggie smiled smugly. 'Much better. And I know I'm doing much better but I can't get that old sober, pessimistic Hartlie to confirm it. I've got an appointment tomorrow. More tests.'

Mark suggested that he drive him to the hospital.

Then Sarah listened as they talked about the coincidental meeting with Barry and the golf courses Mark had managed to get to.

'And did you get to try your hand at snorkeling?' Reggie asked, trying to draw her into the conversation.

'No. Time got away.' She looked down at her hands. 'I never managed to work that in,' she admitted.

'Every time she put on that skimpy suit we seemed to get preoccupied in the room.' Mark's attempt at a joke made her face heat, and, though she wanted to do her 'husband' bodily harm, Reggie loved it.

'Well, maybe the next time,' Reggie assured her.

Then Mark rescued her and she credited a point in his favor to offset the negative one. 'Dad, as much as we've missed you, that flight was long, and the time-change is catching up with me...us,' he amended, yawning then extending his hand. 'If you'll excuse us, Sarah and I need a long nap.'

Reggie chuckled indulgently. 'I'll see you at dinner, then? Well-rested.'

'Sounds good.' Mark ignored the bait and tugged Sarah toward the door.

'Shall I tell Millie eight o'clock?'

'That should be about right,' Mark called.

Sarah had been past the wing where the master suite was, but she'd never been inside the rooms. Millie had promised to move Reggie out and them in while they were gone. If it hadn't been for Reggie's illness she would have protested the change, but she got the impression that neither Millie nor Mark expected Reggie to occupy the rooms again. And Mark had assured her that everything would be much easier this way.

Mark kept hold of her hand until they were out of sight of the open stairs then she gingerly released his and followed him, a pace or so behind, down two long halls.

He finally opened a door with a flourish. 'Welcome home,' he said enigmatically. 'Dad said you could re-furnish this any way you want—actually, he said he thought you'd want to put your own touches on the whole house if we stay here. He wanted me to tell you again that he wouldn't feel deserted or neglected if we want a place of our own.'

And why would we want that? she wondered, staring around the sitting-room that Mark led her into. The room had obviously been modernized over the years, but the foundation for the updates—the extravagantly carved wood moldings, the elegant high ceilings, the huge windows—invited an old-fashioned lingering and cozy tête-à-têtes.

'Moving out would definitely make it easier if you're worried about how we're going to keep anyone from noticing that we aren't sharing quite everything.' She frowned as she noticed that there really wasn't a single piece of furniture in this room that could be comfortably used as a bed. The love-seat was too short, though it seemed to beckon you to grab a book, curl up in the corner and soak up the sun that poured over its woven floral covering. The room also held several bookcases, an antique secretary complete with a replica of an antique phone, and two very comfortable-looking rockers, one of which was draped with a genuinely old knitted blanket.

'The carpet is well-padded,' Mark said. 'Don't consider leaving on my account.' He opened the door into the bedroom and she saw a room dominated by a huge four-poster bed—again a replica, she supposed, since she didn't think that they would have made furniture that size in the days when this one would supposedly have been made. He crossed to a closet and opened that door. Inside was a room half as big again as the bedroom. He pointed out the miles of shelves, long closet-rods, and her few clothes looking lost and lonely in the empty space. 'If nothing else—if you don't mind—I'll sleep in here,' he said.

What could she say? He could sleep anywhere he wanted. She opened another door. 'I see why you can't sleep in your own closet,' she said. The room was a perfect match to the one next to it, but this one was jammed with more clothes than Mark could possibly wear in two lifetimes.

He followed her into his, turning slowly around, staring mostly at the rows and rows of shoes lining three shelves. 'I'll admit it's almost reprehensible,' he said, 'but give you a few months and we'll have yours looking a little more like this.'

She wrapped her arms around her waist and suddenly walked back out. 'I doubt it,' she said. 'I can't imagine what I would do with that many clothes.'

'Wear them,' he said. 'The bathroom's over there.' He nodded toward the door on the opposite side of the room.

'Room' was an understatement. The bathroom was really three smaller rooms, one with a sauna on one side and a step-in whirlpool under windows similar to those in the sitting-room, with a skylight overhead. 'This isn't a bathroom,' she said. 'This is a vacation.'

He was leaning against the door-jamb, watching her in the mirrors lining the wall of sinks and counters and exotic-looking antique jars. 'Why do I get the impression that everything you see pushes you further and further away from me? That you're determined to hold my wealth against me?' he asked, his voice as smoky-smooth as hundred-year-old bourbon.

'I'm not,' she said, starting past him.

He stopped her, his fingers lightly covering her upper arms. 'You are,' he said. 'I'm not Sean,' he added.

'I know that.'

'Every door you've opened in this room has made you stiffer and more brittle. I almost expect you to shatter before my eyes if I say anything too loud.'

'Oh, God, I don't belong here, Mark,' she whispered. 'And I can't imagine how I'm going to keep this up.'

'Remember when I first took you to meet Dad?' he asked.

She looked up at him.

'You remember what I told you then?' He didn't wait for a response this time. 'I said that all you had to do was pretend you liked me—a lot. Remember?'

She nodded.

'Has so much changed?' he asked.

Her mouth suddenly went dry. Her eyes filled with tears. She wanted to bury her head in his shoulder and sob for all she was worth. 'Oh, yes, Mark. It's all changed.'

'How?' he asked gently.

She closed her eyes. He couldn't see them right now. If he did he would know—know how she felt about him. She couldn't afford that humiliation. 'When you asked me to do this ... If you didn't have so much,' she started over, 'it wouldn't be different. But you don't just have things, you have all that history. I can picture generation after generation of distinguished people living in these rooms. I'm terrified I'm going to do something really disastrous and ruin all of that.'

'What? Ruin history?' he chuckled. 'That's something that can't be changed.'

'But it can be rewritten,' she argued. 'Just read a few of the history books they're using now and compare them to the history we studied.'

'Then you have to ask yourself.' He raised her chin with the pressure of one long finger from beneath it. 'Do you care?' He enunciated each word slowly.

'I must do,' she said quietly. 'Otherwise I can't imagine why seeing all this makes me so paranoid.'

His blues eyes warmed her while they held her gaze. 'Oh, I can,' he said. 'It's easy to be paranoid when you're so tired you practically can't see. Let's have that nap we told Dad we were going to take.'

She nodded. 'That's the best suggestion I've heard all day. Can you believe we were in Hawaii just this morning?'

'No,' he agreed. 'It all seems very far away.'

'About two thousand million miles to be exact,' she said, then looked past him toward the bed. 'Where are you going to sleep?'

'With you, I think,' he said, letting his finger move to her lips to waylay her protest. 'Unfortunately, I have the feeling you're going to insist that we sleep. Right?'

She nodded.

'So you look as if you could use a little bit of cuddling and holding. That's all,' he assured her. 'And I'm so exhausted I know I could sleep anywhere, but I'd rather do it comfortably. Who knows when I'll get the chance again?' he added.

How could she disagree? Especially when he bent to remove her shoes as soon as she sat down on the side of the bed. Especially when he lifted her feet, pulled the pillow from beneath the spread and fluffed it for her head. Especially when he unfolded the light-weight quilt over the end of the bed and covered her with it before joining her.

Then his arms felt warm and comforting as they circled her and drew her back against him. And she felt his breath against her hair.

She felt herself relaxing finally. This wasn't going to last forever. She might as well enjoy it while she could.

The dream was one he'd enjoyed frequently enough. The clean scent of Sarah's hair enveloped him. He felt her light touch against his chest. Her breath teased his lips, then her mouth warmed them.

It took him a second to get his eyes open to do a reality check, another to decide that he might as well accept what the gods gave and close them again. Without a bit of effort, he enthusiastically kissed her back.

Her initial response was a startled freeze, her second a groan, then she wrapped the arm that had been against his chest around him, pulling him closer. He didn't resist as she turned on her back, pulling him with her. 'Do we know what we're doing here?' he asked as he settled his weight gently over hers.

'We didn't,' she whispered, and he could hear the pinched tone that told him she was embarrassed. 'But what a pleasant way to wake up.'

'Exactly what I was thinking.'

He gently pushed himself away and glanced at the clock on the end-table. 'It's probably time for us to get up,' he said. 'We've got about twenty minutes until Dad expects us downstairs for dinner.'

He didn't look at her. He knew he wouldn't be able just to go away if she really looked the way she did in the dreams he had dreamed. He headed for a cold shower, trying to ignore the sound of her sigh.

Fortunately for his sanity, the next few days settled quickly into a routine. They both went back to work and Mark managed to be out of the shower, dressed and downstairs before she was up each morning.

He spent each long, uncomfortable, sleepless night on a makeshift bed on the floor of her dressing-room. She protested at first, until he pointed out that his only other option was to sleep in the bed with her. And only in the evenings, with Reggie as an audience, did they actually talk to each other. He had to keep reminding himself that they were only doing this for Reggie. And the effect it was having on his father was nothing short of miraculous.

Reggie's color had returned. His laughter came often and was genuine again. And for some reason he couldn't begin to explain or understand, Mark shied from thinking about Sarah's leaving when all this was finished.

He occasionally reminded himself that it was because to think of Sarah's leaving would be to think of Reggie's death.

Then it came time for Reggie to return to the hospital for another round of tests and chemotherapy. As had been his habit, Mark cleared his court calendar for the day.

'Shall I come with you?' Sarah asked the night before as they were comparing notes in their sitting-room.

He looked up from his book thoughtfully. 'Reggie wouldn't expect it.'

She hesitated a moment by the door of the bedroom. 'I was thinking of you,' she said quietly.

This time he looked up in shock.

'Reggie thinks these treatments are harder on you than him,' she explained. 'He hinted that he thought you might need me there.'

Her tone turned a knife in him. He studied her for a long moment. She had smudges of gray under her usually glowing hazel eyes. Her shoulders drooped wearily. He realized he hadn't heard the gentle laugh or seen the amused smile he'd come to expect from her for days. His book dropped unnoticed to the floor. In two giant strides he was beside her. 'Sarah, what's wrong?'

'Nothing,' she said, surprise and defensiveness in her tone.

'Aren't you sleeping well?' he asked, letting his thumb trace the shadows under her eyes.

'Am I supposed to?' she retorted, the defensiveness a little more dominant now. 'Every time you roll out that ridiculous bedroll in the closet I toss and turn with guilt, knowing I have that huge warm bed, knowing that it's just my stubbornness . . .'

'Are you suggesting we change the arrangements, alter our agreement?' he asked gently.

She shook her head. 'Sometime——' she started, then shook her head again, as if shaking away the words that were at the tip of her tongue. 'Reggie's getting better,' she said. 'Don't you think?'

'I think it's just pure, unadulterated happiness,' he said. 'That's why I'm dreading tomorrow so much.

I'm afraid that reality is all going to come slamming home again and our good times will be over.'

'He's getting better,' she argued. 'Have you thought about what that does to our situation?'

He let his hand rest against her face. 'I'd give anything if that were true.' She leaned almost imperceptibly into the warmth of his palm and his thumb gently traced the contour of her jaw. Her skin was soft, warm. Oh, lord, he wanted to take her in his arms. He dropped his arm to his side.

'You know how much I love your father,' she said. 'I want nothing more than for him to live. But have you thought at all about how long we can continue this if...?'

'With a few minor changes,' he said, 'I could keep this up forever.'

Her eyes narrowed. He resisted the sudden need to smooth away the lines of tension in her forehead. 'I can't,' she said simply, then groped behind her for the doorknob. 'I can't,' she repeated, then fled into the bedroom.

Though her eyes were closed, he knew she wasn't asleep when he came into the room an hour later.

Knowing he was taunting her, knowing that he was torturing himself, he walked slowly to the bedside, smoothed the cornsilk-soft hair away from her forehead. He rearranged the blanket, tucking her in as he might tuck in a child.

If he was lucky his Dad would have a stupendous recovery, and Sarah would be his wife forever. Up until six weeks ago he hadn't been able to face the possibility of losing Reggie. He realized with a terrible jolt that now the stakes had gone up. If he lost Reggie, he'd lose twice.

He suddenly realized that the world really would be a cruel and painfully unusual place to be without her. Then he smiled. He had months, hopefully as much as a year, to convince her that this marriage really should be 'till death—their own—us do part'.

He smiled. He'd bargained with her like a lawyer. He'd bribed her with his worldly goods. Now it was time to seduce her, court her, win her with his love. And he could start now. She was only pretending to sleep. This would give her something to think about as he went to his hard bed on the floor.

The smooth skin on her cheek flinched as his lips brushed it, and he grinned as he walked determinedly away.

One Saturday morning some weeks later, Sarah and Mark stopped for breakfast on the way to the hospital. Mark seemed intent on making her squirm.

She'd ordered an omelet. He'd ordered waffles. He insisted they 'share'. 'In celebration of our two-month anniversary,' he said. 'Well, not exactly,' he amended, when she reminded him that they hadn't been married quite that long yet, 'but it is eight weeks to the day since we met and shared a waffle.'

Then he amused her with the story of how he'd told his father that morning that they'd shared breakfast.

They were at the hospital when Dr Hartlie strolled in like the cat who swallowed the canary.

'What kind of torture have you devised for me today?' Reggie asked weakly, still suffering the after-effects of the barrage of chemicals they'd been filling him with the past two days.

'Oh, I think you'll be interested in this torture,' Hartlie said mysteriously, then invited Mark and Sarah to sit down. He himself sat down on the end of Reggie's bed, crossing his ankles and swinging his feet like a little kid. Then he sighed contentedly, and seemed perfectly willing to let them all stew for a few minutes.

'We've won,' he finally said.

'What?' Reggie and Mark both spoke at once.

'We won,' Dr Hartlie said again. 'At least for now. The tests we did Thursday didn't show a single cell of the cancer. Your lymph nodes are clean. You're in full remission, Barrington,' he added, slapping Reggie's foot happily.

Mark and Reggie both sat with slack jaws. Sarah managed to choke out a question. 'How?'

'We sometimes get lucky,' Hartlie said. 'And the man upstairs must like you,' he added, then launched into a monologue explaining the various fine points of his declaration.

This was one kind of cancer that sometimes responded miraculously—unexpectedly—to the chemotherapy. Reggie would have to continue with the rest of the scheduled treatments and then undergo tests every six months for the next two years. Then they'd do the tests only once every year for the next five. And, though there was no guarantee that there wouldn't eventually be a recurrence, that was often ten, twenty, even thirty years down the road. There was no reason why Reggie couldn't expect to be around to see his grandchildren into adulthood. 'Unless, of course, you do something stupid, like die from old age first,' he added, pleased with his little joke.

Sarah was the first one finally to move.

She jumped from her chair, flung her arms around Reggie's neck, hugging him tight, choking back emotion. Then she ran from the room, sobbing.

It must have been at least half an hour later when Mark sent a nurse into the public rest room down the hall where she'd found refuge to coax her out.

She checked the vicious signs of her emotional outburst in the mirror. Her eyes were red-rimmed, raw-looking. Her hair, which she hadn't pulled back this morning, looked as if it had been attacked by a tornado. Her lips were swollen for some reason. And the tears had left mile-wide tracks down the thin layer of make-up she'd carefully dabbed on this morning. Oh, well. Since she hadn't had the good sense to grab her purse before she'd run maniacally from the room, there wasn't much choice but to face Mark with no protection but clean-washed skin. But, oh, God, her bare face showed too much.

As happy as she was about Reggie, his good news put a death sentence on their marriage. It was no longer necessary. Now Mark had time to find a suitable wife, one he could love with all his heart.

The thoughts started the tears flowing again and she grabbed one of the rough paper towels from the dispenser, held it under the cold water and washed away the tears and scrubbed at the chaotic emotions. By the time she emerged, she felt numb.

Mark stood leaning on the wall opposite the bathroom, one ankle over the other, his arms crossed over his chest. 'Are you okay?' he asked, not moving, his face a mask of inscrutability.

Oh, God, how she wanted to know what he was thinking. She looked up at him sheepishly. 'I'm sorry. I didn't mean to self-destruct like that,' she apologized.

'Why did you?'

He was much too somber. She felt the little bit of hope she carried with her everywhere slowly dissipate. 'It all seemed like too big a tragic joke.' She held out her hands, started to touch him, let them fall idle to her sides. 'I'm delighted about your father,' she added, in case he misunderstood.

He acknowledged her statement with a nod. 'I know.'

'So what do we do now?' she asked.

'Go on.' There wasn't the briefest hesitation in his answer.

'How can we? You can't spend the rest of your life sleeping in the closet.'

'I don't intend to,' he said, finally shoving himself away from the wall. He jammed his fists into the pockets of his baggy multi-pocketed expensive pants. The motion stretched his lightweight sweater taut across his chest.

She froze and focussed on the small bristle of coarse hair that peeked above the V-neck. 'What do you mean?'

'I mean I can't think of a single reason not to just quit playing at this marriage and go on as if we intend to make it permanent.'

'How can we?' she asked again.

'A lot of successful marriages have probably been founded on a lot less.'

Her mouth felt dry. 'A lot less than what?'

'Financial security.'

This time she flinched.

'Emotional need.'

Hope sparked, then died almost as quickly as it had risen. The grim expression on his face didn't denote even a hint of the 'emotional need' she'd grasped at for a moment. 'Do you want to explain that?' she asked, hating herself for not accepting his words at face value.

'You helped me fill an emotional need. I'm not going to back out of our agreement simply because the need is no longer valid.'

'And what about love?' she asked, obviously determined to torture herself. 'Don't you ever hope to have it? Wouldn't you eventually like a marriage based on that magic you father glows with when he talks about your mother?'

'Until lately I've never really thought much about it. I imagine I'll do just fine if I have to live without it,' he said, effectively killing the last bit of optimism she was holding on to.

'No.' She turned and strode down the hall toward the elevator.

Mark started after her. She heard his heavy tread behind her. 'What do you mean?'

'I mean I don't want life in a vacuum. I want everything. I came here to *get* everything. I'm not going to settle for what you're talking about. I want success that someone hasn't handed to me, a home that I don't feel like some kind of a parasite in. And I want a marriage and kids that have nothing to do with necessity and everything to do with the way I feel in here.' She thumped her heart with her fist, realized he couldn't see since he was following her, but decided it didn't matter. Surely he'd got her message loud and clear. She just prayed he hadn't seen through everything, that it wasn't obvious that everything she wanted she wanted with him—but not without love. So far, the taste of that was very bitter.

Several of the staff stole furtive glances at them as they passed the nurses' station and all conversation stopped. They'd obviously been watching the drama, discussing it in hushed voices. Sarah felt herself flush, but kept right on going.

Mark caught her as she punched the 'down' button at the elevator's closed doors. He lightly grasped her wrist, turning her around.

'Sarah.'

'We've got to tell him, Mark.' She stared at his long fingers, tan against her pale skin, and wondered idly how he could send those shimmers of excitement through her with just a simple touch.

'I won't,' he said bluntly. 'Did you ever consider that the feelings could grow if we give them a chance? You like me, don't you? We like each other. That's surely a start. And in a lot of cultures, including this one for many, many years, arranged marriages——'

The elevator doors slid open and a patient in hospital garb and her visitor sidestepped past them.

Sarah twisted her arm and Mark let her go. She hurried on just as the elevator doors started to close. They slid wide again and Sarah stood gazing at him. 'You dad is going to be fine, Mark. Now we have to get on with our lives,' she said as they finally slid closed to separate them.

CHAPTER TEN

REGGIE was coming home two days later. Sarah made sure she was gone before he and Mark were scheduled to arrive from the hospital.

She took a taxi to her new and barren home. An hour later she was 'unpacked', and pleased with how well she'd done in the short period of time she'd had to find the new apartment. Even Mark would be pleasantly surprised, she thought.

It was a one-room studio, plain, functional and clean, with a furnished kitchenette. And it was only three blocks from a major subway station—and a world away from both the neighborhood Mark had been so horrified to find her in two months ago and his wealthy suburban one.

With nearly five and a half thousand dollars in the bank now, she was fairly sure she could maintain the simple lifestyle—especially if she took a second job. And now she needed that as much to keep herself busy as she needed it for the money.

She sat down with a freshly brewed cup of coffee and scanned the ads. With a city map in one hand, she half-heartedly circled restaurants within walking distance of her new address and whole-heartedly dreaded going to work tomorrow. Breaking the news that she was separated from her new husband would not be easy.

No doubt someone would win a pool somewhere in the huge building where she and her marriage to Mark had become the hottest gossip since the last government scandal.

'They'll think I had a miscarriage, or found out I wasn't really pregnant after all,' she muttered to herself as she marked another job prospect. She'd seen the calendar in the copy-room, initialed by more than a few of her fellow employees on various dates—all within the next six or seven months.

Too bad they hadn't taken bets on how long the shortest marriage in history would last instead, she thought with a wry smile, but without a shred of amusement.

Geminy! What was she doing here? And how was she going to keep from thinking of Mark? A permanent ache had settled in her chest and she already felt her sanity slipping. All she could think of was what Reggie would think. Would he forgive her when he found her note?

And Mark. What would he think? What would he do when he found her gone?

And the only trail she'd left him was through work—supposing he had any desire to find her.

She dropped her pencil and gave up trying to concentrate.

Three months later not a thing had changed. She worked, she waited tables at the little Cuban restaurant down the street, and existed. And Mark hadn't even tried to contact her, except for a short note he'd sent via the office accompanying the legal papers he said she could file as soon as she wanted the annulment. She'd received another couple of packets of forwarded mail before she'd got around to telling her family and friends about her broken marriage and Reggie's good news, but never a personal word from either of them.

For a few weeks she'd convinced herself that she hadn't filed them simply because she hadn't had time without taking an afternoon off work. She'd admitted that wasn't true shortly after, and now she wasn't at all sure *why* she hadn't taken any measures to end the marriage that never should have been.

No. That wasn't true. At the time Reggie had needed their marriage. And, whatever medical evidence anyone could have produced, she would never believe anything but that they'd played a very big part in her father-in-law's remission. It was the only way she could live with the lie she and Mark had created.

And now, at five o'clock on a Saturday afternoon, she decided it was time she made her peace with them.

An hour and forty-five minutes later her taxi pulled up outside the gates of the mansion Mark had said had been in his mother's family for three generations—four, counting him.

'Millie?' she said tentatively into the speaker outside, when a woman answered her buzz.

'Who's asking?' Millie said in her most indignant voice.

'It's Sarah,' she replied, and heard a masculine curse in the background.

'Sarah?' Reggie's voice came over the little box and the gates immediately began to swing open. 'For heaven's sake, child, you should have called. I would have had the gates open. Get yourself up here.'

The cab-driver eyed her in the rearview mirror, and with shaking hands she dug in her purse for money to pay him as he shot the car up the long, winter-drab drive.

What was she going to say? She felt her face heating and suddenly was sure she had a raging temperature. She was coming down with some virulent form of flu. She shouldn't be here. She had to concentrate on the still ticking meter to keep from urging the driver to turn around.

The double doors of the house flew open before the car came to a complete stop. Sarah handed the man his money as Reggie yanked open her door and hauled her out, pulling her right into his warm embrace.

She let his rough and tight hug warm her. His gruff, 'Sarah,' calmed the shaking that she blamed on the near-freezing weather. And finally she steeled up enough nerve to open her eyes and look over Reggie's shoulder. She wasn't sure if the emotion that swept her was relief or despair. Mark wasn't anywhere to be seen. Millie was, though, and she waved from the doorway.

'Come in,' Reggie said as the taxi moved on around the circle and back down the drive. 'We're both going to freeze to death.'

He didn't have a coat on, she realized guiltily. His ears were already pink from the cold. She wasn't sure who hustled whom into the house.

'Nice to see you again, Sarah,' Millie said formally, a mixture of caution and sincerity in her voice as she closed the door behind them.

'Nice to see you, Millie.'

'Come into the den,' Reggie said, still holding her hand. 'Millie, why don't you get us some...?' He looked to Sarah. 'Hot chocolate?' he said.

'That sounds wonderful,' she said as he led her into the room where she had stood—over by the windows in the sun—vowing to love, honor and cherish Mark.

A stab of regret hit her so unexpectedly that she had to fight the pain. Regret for what? Regret that Mark didn't love her? Regret that she hadn't taken him up on his offer and held on to him despite the fact that what he had proposed was as cold and emotionless and without love as their decision to marry in the first place? More than once in these last few months she had wondered what would have happened if she'd just 'let nature take its course'.

Reggie interrupted her thoughts, stepping away from her. 'Let me look at you,' he said, holding her hands wide as he checked her out.

She took the opportunity to examine him, too. He'd gained a little weight. His lined face held a plump, slightly pink, healthy sheen. And, surprisingly, he looked a little younger—except his eyes. They still held the sadness she had recognized the first time they'd met. She knew instinctively that at least part of that was her fault.

'You've lost weight,' Reggie rebuked her, helping her out of her coat.

She shrugged and Millie brought in the tray with hot chocolate.

'This will help,' he said. 'Millie uses nothing but cream in her hot chocolate. It's nothing more than cholesterol and pure bliss.' He thanked Millie and handed her Sarah's coat and gloves. 'And while

Millie's here I might as well go ahead and ask if you will join me for dinner.'

'Where's Mark?' Sarah had to ask eventually, and decided it might as well be now, before she committed herself.

Millie stiffened, clearing her throat awkwardly.

'He had an engagement,' Reggie answered gently, his eyes wide, his brows raised. His expression told her frankly what type of engagement it was. 'I would truly love to have your company.'

Sarah said, 'And I would love to join you.'

Millie smiled approvingly and headed for the door. 'Dinner will be in about an hour,' she said.

As soon as she was gone, Reggie invited Sarah to sit. The den that had been sunny and bright during the fall had taken on winter's gloom. Each corner of the room was shadowed; the heavy drapes were pulled to keep out the chilly drafts, but a fire crackled mellowly in the huge fireplace.

'So, tell me why you left,' Reggie said as he sat down in the wing chair across from her. 'Mark finally admitted the whole marriage had been a sham from start to finish, but not till I indicated that I had guessed. He also said he hadn't been averse to carrying on. So why did you leave?'

'Wouldn't you want Mark to have the kind of marriage you and your wife had?' she asked simply. 'Mark doesn't love me. It was better to end it while everyone was happy rather than wait until we were all well and firmly trapped and miserable.'

'Were you miserable?' Reggie asked, true caring in his voice.

'No.'

'Are you happy now?'

'No,' she whispered. 'But I feel good about myself again. I'm not relying on Mark—or you—to keep me from self-destructing in this city.'

Reggie chuckled softly. 'Is that how you felt?'

She nodded. 'Didn't Mark tell you everything that led up to our engagement?'

'He'd told me a lot of it before you were married. The only thing he failed to mention was that it was for me. None of it was for either of you.'

She felt like crying. Instead impulsively she closed the short space between them and hugged him. 'Thank you for understanding.'

'I don't really. I wish you'd see Mark,' he said, returning the hug, stroking and patting her back. 'Talk to him. I'm not convinced that this break-up was for the best for either of you. You care for him, don't you?'

'I married him for money,' she protested, rocking back on her heels and kneeling comfortably on the floor in front of him. 'I'll never fit into his life. And then we come back to the subject of love.' She glanced down at her fingers. 'Someday I hope to marry for love.'

'I can understand that too.' Reggie didn't say another word on the subject. They talked about her job, his health, everything under the sun except Mark after that.

When the simple but filling meal was finished Mark still hadn't returned from his date. She didn't want to be here when he did, she decided.

Reggie called a cab while Millie brought Sarah's coat and packed her the leftover chicken pot pie from dinner. 'You obviously aren't eating right.' Millie handed her the foil-covered pan. 'You take this. It'll just go to waste here.'

Reggie made her promise to keep in touch, writing down her new phone number and address while they waited for her ride. 'You just remember that whatever happened—or didn't—between you and Mark, I consider you a very dear friend. I'm here if you need me.'

She gave him her assurance.

'And Sarah, it's okay to cherish your independence, but remember that no one, and I truly mean no one, ever makes it totally on his or her own. We all need other people. There's nothing wrong with that.'

His words were like a revelation. Reggie was right. She wondered at what point she'd forgotten that there was nothing wrong with needing other people. With a final hug she was on her way, the lonely ache in her heart soothed a little for now. But a new ache was well-established.

Whether or not Mark had loved her, he'd needed her. And she was realizing it too late.

Mark was seeing someone else.

She'd barely been back at her apartment half an hour when someone knocked on the door. That happened so rarely that habit and curiosity kicked in before common sense.

'What in the hell are you doing?' Mark started lecturing as soon as she opened the door. 'Don't you *ever* check who's at the door before you open it? Good lord, Sarah, this is Washington, DC.'

'Mark.' Oh, God, she was happy to see him—even if he was still his arrogant, dictatorial self. His dark hair was tousled by the winter wind, and a few flecks of the snow that had begun to spit while she was on her way home still clung to his hair.

He pushed past her, not waiting for her to invite him in. 'Dad said you came by the house tonight.'

She nodded, blinking like an owl as she tried to focus on what he was saying instead of on her shock and joy at seeing him again.

'Mark,' she said again, this time in a whisper. His mouth and his straight, strong nose were reddened by the cold. The collar of his long dark coat was turned up around his ears, which had also been nipped by the frosty weather, and her fingers moved automatically to cradle and warm them.

He leaned away from her touch and stepped around her. 'I take it you came to see what we need to do next about the annulment.'

That brought her out of her daze. 'I suppose that would be a good idea,' she said, remembering where he had been tonight. 'But you gave fairly clear instructions in the note you included when you sent the papers. I imagine you're ready to get on with your life. Reggie said you had a date this evening.'

'I never stopped living mine,' he said. His eyes glimmered dangerously as he stepped a half-pace closer. 'You're the one who has seemed so intent on keeping everything about our marriage totally segregated from the rest of your life.'

She backed up. 'I didn't want to take advantage. I didn't want you to feel obligated——'

'I do. I did,' he amended. 'I've felt obligated to you since that first day in the restaurant when you first made me laugh.'

She frowned. Since she made him laugh? Not since he'd quit her job and found out she was destitute?

His hands closed around her upper arms. 'You were never a kept woman,' he said ruefully. 'However much I wished it. You gave Dad and me so much more than we ever gave you. You gave him hope and you gave me...' He let the unfinished sentence linger in the air between them.

'What? What did I give you?' she asked, afraid of the answer, hurting because the hope that their marriage had given his father had been all she could offer to Mark, too.

'You gave me back my emotions,' he finally said.

His hands slowly dropped to his sides and he impatiently buried them in his pockets, stretching his coat taut over his shoulders.

'Oh, yeah, I've given you such a wonderful range of emotions: anger, irritation, impatience, a few good chuckles——'

'Feeling anger, frustration—feeling anything—was a nice change of pace for me. Sarah, don't you realize how numb I had become? Part of it, I'm sure, was from listening to the things I hear day after day. I've learned to barricade my feelings so my contempt or sorrow for the wasted lives I see doesn't interfere with my objectivity. Otherwise I would make too many mistakes. That's why I thought I was a good judge.'

'You are a good judge. At the wedding lots of people told me how proud I should be of you.'

'I'm better now,' he contradicted. 'I didn't comprehend what a difference being raised in various cultures, without a woman's emotional touch, had made in me until you entered my life.'

'But you and your father——'

'My father has always given me lots of love, but until I thought I would lose him I didn't realize how little I'd given back. In fact, until Dad got sick, I'd never felt comfortable showing him affection. It was there and he knew it, but it wasn't verbalized or acted upon. We shared long, philosophical discussions and wrestled around in the yard when I was younger, but he hadn't actually told me that he loved me since the day he sent me back to the States to enrol in high school while he finished his stint at the embassy in Syria. He knew we wouldn't see each other for almost four months.'

'Oh, Mark, I can't believe that.'

'Why? Relationships during those growing-up years were temporary, so I enjoyed them while I had them and learned to replace them quickly when they were gone.'

She had to look away. That was what he was doing now, she realized, replacing their relationship with a new one.

'You don't much want to hear this, do you?' he asked.

'I don't understand how it helps us much now.'

'I promised myself I would say it all when I came here. Whatever you think about what I have to say, it will help me.'

She bit her lip as he looked around, taking in her sparsely furnished apartment. 'Call it therapy, if you want. I promised myself I would say everything I needed to before I leave,' he said, striding for the small kitchen tucked in one corner of the room and helping himself to one of the mugs on the stand by the coffee-pot. 'May I?' he asked. Without waiting for an answer he poured himself a cup of her fresh coffee and sat down on the high stool at the kitchen counter where she ate most of her meals.

She forced her legs to carry her across the room and refilled her own cup, taking it to the only other seating in the place. She sagged on to the edge of the bed.

'Still don't have much furniture,' he commented, blowing on the coffee.

'No, I plan to buy myself an easy chair soon,' she said.

He raised an eyebrow. 'Have you been home lately?'

'No.'

'What did you do for Christmas?' he asked.

'Worked.'

He scowled.

'I have another job—at a little restaurant a couple of blocks from here,' she explained. 'They were open.'

'You surely don't need the money that desperately again?'

'Not that it's any of your business, but I don't plan to *get* in that shape again. And that's why I'll be able to afford a comfortable chair for my apartment after I get paid next week.'

She had leaned her elbows on her knees and was staring pointedly into her cup, so she didn't realize he had left his chair until the tops of his shoes came into her circle of vision. She looked up, startled, as he stopped in front of her.

'You're wrong,' he said between clenched teeth. 'It is my business. We're still married, however hard you try to pretend we're not. And if you need money——'

'Everyone needs money,' she interrupted. 'But I don't need yours.'

'All I want to do is help,' he said. 'Can't I do that for my wife?'

'Get it annulled, Mark.' She sat her mug on the end-table beside the bed. 'Finish the legalities so you can be done with the guilt. Look around you, Mark, I'm doing fine.' She touched his hand imploringly and he went still. His focus on her fingers made them feel hot and laced with nervous jolts. She would have withdrawn the gesture but his hand circled hers.

'Your hand looks strange without Mom's rings.'

'I know,' she agreed, and looked up and into his eyes.

His gaze hungrily searched her face. 'You look good,' he said. 'Dad said you'd lost weight.'

'I needed to lose a few pounds,' she said. 'All that rich food on our honeymoon——' Geminy Christmas, why did she have to bring that up? And the way he was looking at her mouth...

She nervously licked her lips. 'So who are you seeing now?' she asked, and groaned inwardly. She didn't want to know, though she supposed it would be good for him to see that it didn't bother her.

'I played tennis and had dinner with a lawyer who represented someone in my court a couple of weeks ago.'

'Did she win?'

'The case or the tennis?' he asked. 'She won both,' he answered before she could.

'Sounds like exactly the type of person you need,' she said. 'I'm sure you have a lot in comm——'

'I won't be seeing her again,' he cut her comment short.

'Why?'

He concentrated on entwining his fingers with hers. 'I'm still in love with my wife,' he said, not looking at her.

She knew her mouth dropped open. She knew her heart was clamoring so noisily he could probably hear it. She knew he had to be joking. Her lips were suddenly as dry as the August wind in Kansas. She wet them again. 'I think you have a very impressive imagination. It's guilt. You don't love me.'

'And how do you know that?' With the knuckles of his free hand he gently chucked her beneath the chin.

'You can't...' She was making a colossal fool of herself again. 'You need to marry someone who could...who would...' She couldn't describe the person he needed. A burning pain shot through her just trying. She just knew it wasn't her.

'That would be pretty tricky,' he said, chuckling. 'They frown on taking more than one wife in every state in the union except one. This isn't the one.'

She felt the hated heat rising in her cheeks. 'That's why you need to have our marriage annulled.'

'Oh, God, Sarah,' he groaned, closing his eyes, pulling her to her feet and wrapping her tightly in an embrace. 'Do you know how much I need you? I've barely smiled, let alone laughed since you left. I love you, Sarah. Won't you please listen to me with your heart for a minute instead of your head?'

'If it's true, why didn't you tell me?'

'I thought I had.' He held her away from him, searching her face as he said what he needed to say. 'I thought I had told you in every way possible how much I loved you.'

'No, you didn't,' she protested, wary of letting what he was saying sink in.

'I didn't think to say the words.' He sighed deeply and shook his head. 'When you kept insisting that you'd married me because you needed the money, and hinted that you felt you were prostituting yourself, it never occurred to me that love was even an issue. At least not until Dad assumed tonight that I loved you and told me just to be patient. He thinks you love me too,' he added, his dark eyes seeking answers in hers. 'It hit me like a ton of bricks that I'd never actually said it. I'm saying it now. It's what I came here to say. I love you, Sarah.'

She wanted to listen with her heart, let it soar as it was trying to do. 'But I don't fit, Mark,' she said, gulping a deep breath of reality. 'I felt as terrible for you when you were ashamed of me as I did for me. How can——?'

'What are you talking about?' He pushed her an arm's length away. His voice was as incredulous as when he'd lectured her when he'd come in the door.

'You didn't want to be seen with me those last few days in Hawaii, and I don't blame you. You avoided me. I don't have—— '

'My God. That's what you thought?'

'I know I don't have all the social graces and the wonderful clothes and——'

This time he crushed her to him until she thought her bones would pop.

'I avoided you because I wasn't sure how much longer I could keep my hands off you. You made it perfectly clear that you didn't want to complicate our non-marriage with sex.' He closed his eyes and shook his head. 'Good God, Sarah, I avoided you like the plague because I didn't know what I might do if I spent one more second alone with you.' He opened his eyes again, trapping hers with a steady gaze. 'Do you know the panic I felt when you proposed that we go snorkeling?' He didn't wait for her to respond. 'The two of us? Alone? On some deserted strip of beach with you in one of those almost-nothing swim-suits? I practically had to run out of the room thinking about it.'

She smiled. She couldn't help it. 'Maybe you should have agreed. Maybe that was exactly what we needed.'

'Maybe. I didn't dare take the chance. I would have done this.' He pecked a kiss on her cheek. 'Then this.' This kiss was softer, lingering. His fingers slowly traced the curves of her back, the entire length of her body. The almost whispery touch left her breathless and tingling. 'And then probably this.' His hand slipped beneath the hem of her sweater and molded itself to her bare skin. 'Oh, God, Sarah, I wanted to touch you.'

His lips covered hers with a kiss that started at bittersweet and graduated to passionate.

He finally lifted his head. 'And, had you responded like that, it would have taken an earthquake to stop what comes next.'

Sarah's limbs felt lifeless. She had to concentrate to stay standing on her feet.

'I hadn't admitted to myself that I loved you by then, but I knew I didn't want to rush you, to scare you away.'

'When did you know?' she managed to ask despite gasping for air.

'The day you came in with that womanizing pilot.'

His description of Jim made her laugh.

He looked at her with a mock-warning at her amusement. 'That whole trip was the closest thing to hell I ever want to experience.'

Sarah allowed herself to hope, to let her heart rise in anticipation. 'You love me?' The words held all her wonder at the thought.

'With all my heart and soul and spirit. But I still like the idea of showing rather than telling you. And I think it's your turn. Haven't I suffered enough? Do you love me?' he asked gruffly, holding her away for a second.

'Oh, Mark, I shouldn't, but I do.' Her palms cradled his face and his lips suddenly looked so inviting that she was sure that if he didn't kiss her soon she would waste away from the deprivation.

'Why shouldn't you?' he asked. 'Why in hell shouldn't you love me? What is *wrong* with loving me?' His grip on her arms tightened almost painfully.

'You could do so much better,' she whispered. 'The lady lawyer, for instance. She sounds perf——'

'She didn't make me smile or feel anything even once today—except maybe how much I wanted her to be you. You would sentence me to a life of feeling nothing?'

The remembered pain, the hopeful longing displayed so clearly on his face sparked her own joy to life at last. 'And what was that feeling you said you had for me?' she whispered teasingly.

He laughed and happiness welled up in her chest as he pulled her so close that the laughter could have come from either of them.

'Love, Sarah,' he assured her. 'I feel love. I'll say it as many times as you want me to if you will just say it once without adding "I shouldn't".'

'I love you, Mark,' she said sincerely. 'But if you don't kiss me soon I'm going to die, so loving you won't do me or you much good.'

His eyelids closed lazily. 'We're back to that, huh?' He sighed against her mouth.

Heaven. She'd died and gone to heaven. 'Back to what?' she responded in the same strange braille where the words were felt as much as heard.

He didn't answer. Instead he deepened the kiss.

For a long, long time she didn't think, or say, or feel anything except his mouth against hers, the weight of his body as he laid her gently on the bed, then skin against skin as they slowly, certainly rid themselves of every last remnant separating them.

'Make love to me, Mark,' she finally begged.

He hesitated, cradling, sheltering her against his chest. 'Not until you say it again. This time, just for us,' he said, spreading kisses over her eyelids, her cheeks, the tip of her nose. 'I can't endure the thought of waking up tomorrow or the next day or the next and finding out this was just another dream.'

'You're awake,' she promised, with a gentle pinch on his shoulder that needed an immediate kiss to make it better. 'But I don't have any idea what you're talking about.'

God. How could he expect her to carry on an intelligent conversation when he was making it impossible to think? She gasped as his tongue teased its way to the tip of her breast.

'You'll have to promise to love, honor, cherish me all over again.' This time she tortured him, and he groaned. 'Till death us do part,' he managed to add.

'Would you settle for forever?' she whispered, slowly losing her mind as he cast his magic all over again.

'Forever sounds fine,' he said.

And slowly, surely, he made her wonder if forever was long enough.

FLYAWAY VACATION SWEEPSTAKES!

This month's destination:

Exciting ORLANDO, FLORIDA!

Are you the lucky person who will win a free trip to Orlando? Imagine how much fun it would be to visit Walt Disney World**, Universal Studios**, Cape Canaveral and the other sights and attractions in this area! The Next page contains tow Official Entry Coupons, as does each of the other books you received this shipment. Complete and return *all* the entry coupons—the more times you enter, the better your chances of winning!

Then keep your fingers crossed, because you'll find out by October 15, 1995 if you're the winner! If you are, here's what you'll get:

- Round-trip airfare for two to Orlando!
- 4 days/3 nights at a first-class resort hotel!
- $500.00 pocket money for meals and sightseeing!

Remember: The more times you enter, the better your chances of winning!*

*NO PURCHASE OR OBLIGATION TO CONTINUE BEING A SUBSCRIBER NECESSARY TO ENTER. SEE BACK PAGE FOR ALTERNATIVE MEANS OF ENTRY AND RULES.

**THE PROPRIETORS OF THE TRADEMARKS ARE NOT ASSOCIATED WITH THIS PROMOTION.

VOR KAL

▰▰▰ FLYAWAY VACATION ▰▰▰
SWEEPSTAKES
OFFICIAL ENTRY COUPON

This entry must be received by: SEPTEMBER 30, 1995
This month's winner will be notified by: OCTOBER 15, 1995
Trip must be taken between: NOVEMBER 30, 1995-NOVEMBER 30, 1996

YES, I want to win the vacation for two to Orlando, Florida. I understand the prize includes round-trip airfare, first-class hotel and $500.00 spending money. Please let me know if I'm the winner!

Name_____

Address _____ Apt. _____

_____
City   State/Prov.   Zip/Postal Code

Account #_____

Return entry with invoice in reply envelope.

© 1995 HARLEQUIN ENTERPRISES LTD.   COR KAL

▰▰▰ FLYAWAY VACATION ▰▰▰
SWEEPSTAKES
OFFICIAL ENTRY COUPON

This entry must be received by: SEPTEMBER 30, 1995
This month's winner will be notified by: OCTOBER 15, 1995
Trip must be taken between: NOVEMBER 30, 1995-NOVEMBER 30, 1996

YES, I want to win the vacation for two to Orlando, Florida. I understand the prize includes round-trip airfare, first-class hotel and $500.00 spending money. Please let me know if I'm the winner!

Name_____

Address _____ Apt. _____

_____
City   State/Prov.   Zip/Postal Code

Account #_____

Return entry with invoice in reply envelope.

© 1995 HARLEQUIN ENTERPRISES LTD.   COR KAL

OFFICIAL RULES

FLYAWAY VACATION SWEEPSTAKES 3449

NO PURCHASE OR OBLIGATION NECESSARY

Three Harlequin Reader Service 1995 shipments will contain respectively, coupons for entry into three different prize drawings, one for a trip for two to San Francisco, another for a trip for two to Las Vegas and the third for a trip for two to Orlando, Florida. To enter any drawing using an Entry Coupon, simply complete and mail according to directions.

There is no obligation to continue using the Reader Service to enter and be eligible for any prize drawing. You may also enter any drawing by hand printing the words "Flyaway Vacation," your name and address on a 3"x5" card and the destination of the prize you wish that entry to be considered for (i.e., San Francisco trip, Las Vegas trip or Orlando trip). Send your 3"x5" entries via first-class mail (limit: one entry per envelope) to: Flyaway Vacation Sweepstakes 3449, c/o Prize Destination you wish that entry to be considered for, P.O. Box 1315, Buffalo, NY 14269-1315, USA or P.O. Box 610, Fort Erie, Ontario L2A 5X3, Canada.

To be eligible for the San Francisco trip, entries must be received by 5/30/95; for the Las Vegas trip, 7/30/95; and for the Orlando trip, 9/30/95.

Winners will be determined in random drawings conducted under the supervision of D.L. Blair, Inc., an independent judging organization whose decisions are final, from among all eligible entries received for that drawing. San Francisco trip prize includes round-trip airfare for two, 4-day/3-night weekend accommodations at a first-class hotel, and $500 in cash (trip must be taken between 7/30/95—7/30/96, approximate prize value—$3,500); Las Vegas trip includes round-trip airfare for two, 4-day/3-night weekend accommodations at a first-class hotel, and $500 in cash (trip must be taken between 9/30/95—9/30/96, approximate prize value—$3,500); Orlando trip includes round-trip airfare for two, 4-day/3-night weekend accommodations at a first-class hotel, and $500 in cash (trip must be taken between 11/30/95—11/30/96, approximate prize value—$3,500). All travelers must sign and return a Release of Liability prior to travel. Hotel accommodations and flights are subject to accommodation and schedule availability. Sweepstakes open to residents of the U.S. (except Puerto Rico) and Canada, 18 years of age or older. Employees and immediate family members of Harlequin Enterprises, Ltd., D.L. Blair, Inc., their affiliates, subsidiaries and all other agencies, entities and persons connected with the use, marketing or conduct of this sweepstakes are not eligible. Odds of winning a prize are dependent upon the number of eligible entries received for that drawing. Prize drawing and winner notification for each drawing will occur no later than 15 days after deadline for entry eligibility for that drawing. Limit: one prize to an individual, family or organization. All applicable laws and regulations apply. Sweepstakes offer void wherever prohibited by law. Any litigation within the province of Quebec respecting the conduct and awarding of the prizes in this sweepstakes must be submitted to the Regies des loteries et Courses du Quebec. In order to win a prize, residents of Canada will be required to correctly answer a time-limited arithmetical skill-testing question. Value of prizes are in U.S. currency.

Winners will be obligated to sign and return an Affidavit of Eligibility within 30 days of notification. In the event of noncompliance within this time period, prize may not be awarded. If any prize or prize notification is returned as undeliverable, that prize will not be awarded. By acceptance of a prize, winner consents to use of his/her name, photograph or other likeness for purposes of advertising, trade and promotion on behalf of Harlequin Enterprises, Ltd., without further compensation, unless prohibited by law.

For the names of prizewinners (available after 12/31/95), send a self-addressed, stamped envelope to: Flyaway Vacation Sweepstakes 3449 Winners, P.O. Box 4200, Blair, NE 68009.

RVC KAL